"Care to dance?"

As Mac swept her into his arms and began to dance, she forgot about her fear she'd be exposed and escorted from the ball. She could only see Mac, smell the enticing scent of his aftershave, relish the strength of the muscles beneath his jacket.

His dark eyes were mesmerizing. Seconds spun by. She wanted to trace that slight dimple in his left cheek. Wanted to shift her hand from his shoulder to his neck and feel the warmth of his skin. She wanted to learn more about the stranger with whom she danced so superbly. The night was full of magic and she savored every moment. All too soon it would end and she'd be back to her day-to-day routine.

She knew she was on borrowed time. But a few stolen moments of dancing with Mac were worth any risk.

Barbara McMahon was born and raised in the South, but settled in California after spending a year flying around the world for an international airline. After settling down to raise a family and work for a computer firm, she began writing when her children started school. Now, feeling fortunate in being able to realise a long-held dream of quitting her 'day job' and writing full time, she and her husband have moved to the Sierra Nevada mountains of California, where she finds her desire to write is stronger than ever. With the beauty of the mountains visible from her windows, and the pace of life slower than the hectic San Francisco Bay Area where they previously resided, she finds more time than ever to think up stories and characters and share them with others through writing. Barbara loves to hear from readers. You can reach her at PO Box 977, Pioneer, CA 95666-0977, USA. Readers can also contact Barbara at her website: www.barbaramcmahon.com

NANNY TO THE BILLIONAIRE'S SON

BY
BARBARA McMAHON

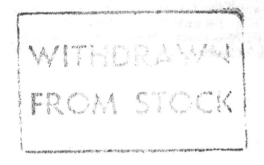

MILLS & BOON®
Pure reading pleasure™

First published in Great Britain 2008
Harlequin Mills & Boon Limited,
Eton House, 18-24 Paradise Road, Richmond, Surrey TW9 1SR

© Barbara McMahon 2008

ISBN: 978 0 263 20390 5

Set in Times Roman 10½ on 11½ pt
07-1108-55841

Printed and bound in Great Britain
by CPI Antony Rowe, Chippenham, Wiltshire

NANNY TO THE
BILLIONAIRE'S SON

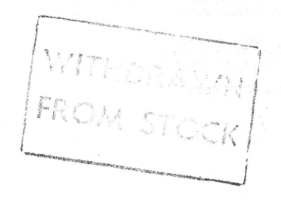

Chuck Nash, for always being there for me.
I love you, Daddy.

PROLOGUE

SAMANTHA DUNCAN lifted the crumpled card from the floor. It had fluttered in the air when she dumped the deskside trash can. Smoothing it out on the flat surface of the mahogany desk, her fingers traced the embossed print, complete with gold emblem at the top. It was a ticket to Atlanta's Black and White Ball on New Year's Eve. The thick, creamy paper screamed expensive, as did the fancy script. Of course tickets to the ball went at five hundred dollars a pop, so they should look elegant.

And the owner of this one had crumpled it up and tossed it away. For a moment her imagination sparked. She'd love to go to a ball, dressed to the nines, flirt with dashing captains of industry, or trust-fund men who never had to work two jobs to make ends meet.

She held it over the large barrel that held the floor's trash, hesitated a moment, then slid it in her apron pocket, righted the trash container and continued with the task of dusting and vacuuming the office of the CEO of McAlheny Industries. It probably meant nothing to the man. He was one of the top-ten wealthiest men in Atlanta, maybe even the East Coast. A mere five hundred dollars would be a pittance to him.

As she worked, she furthered her image of herself at the ball, just like Cinderella. She'd be wearing a fabulous designer creation. Men would fall over themselves asking her to dance. She wouldn't sit out a single one. And she would be dazzling in her witty repartee.

The food was rumored to be to die for. She had a sweet tooth and couldn't help wondering, would the desserts be beyond fabulous? She'd love to have crème brûlée or a super-rich chocolate torte.

"Ready to move to the next floor?" One of her coworkers waited at the door. Sam glanced around the pristine office and nodded. The bubble popped. She was tired. The good news was she only had another five offices on the next floor to clean and she'd be finished for the evening.

It was hard to work all day at her regular job then put in six hours cleaning offices, but she needed the money in the worst way. She'd been lucky to get this job. Still, it was Friday night. Once finished, she'd have two days to sleep in, nap and get ready for the next workweek.

Not for her the promise of a Cinderella ball. She knew her limitations. After Chad, she knew better than to daydream about men dropping at her feet. The reality was always there to face as soon as they met Charlene.

Saturday morning Sam slept in until nine. Not super late, but late enough for someone who usually rose before seven and was at work by eight.

She donned on her robe, slipping the ticket in her pocket, and went downstairs. Her sister was in the small study she used as her office, typing away. Sam paused at the door.

"Did you eat already?"

Charlene looked up and shook her head. "I waited for you. I was hoping for blueberry pancakes."

"Sounds good," Sam said. She headed for the kitchen. Feeling slightly depressed when she entered, she glanced at the patched wall where the old oak tree had crashed through during Hurricane George. The damage remained, awaiting funds to repair it. Sighing softly, she quickly moved to gather ingredients to make the pancake batter, using the small, two-burner camp stove they were making do with. Once she had enough money, they would get the kitchen repaired and at that point she was buying a top-of-the-line gas range.

Charlene rolled into the kitchen.

"Want any help?" she asked.

"No, I've got it. Why are you working on Saturday? I thought you tried to get everything done during the week."

"I know, but I got caught up in quilting on Thursday and so am behind a bit. I need to be caught up by Monday." Charlene was a medical transcriptionist for a local physicians' clinic. She worked at home and normally her income plus Sam's kept them afloat. The hurricane had caused them to dip into their small savings, and still repairs remained waiting to be done.

"Oh, look what I brought home," Sam said, pulling the invitation from her robe pocket and tossing it to her sister.

"Pretty," Charlene said, looking at it. "I didn't know you got a ticket."

"I didn't. It fell out of the trash at one of the offices last night. I brought it home for you to see. Really posh, don't you think?"

Charlene toyed with it, glancing at Sam from time to time as Sam flipped the pancakes and dished them up. As soon as Sam sat, Charlene said, "You should go."

"Where?"

"To the ball, of course." She tapped the edge of the invitation on the table. "It's obviously not being used by anyone."

"Someone paid big bucks for that. I can't use it," Sam pointed out, pouring on the maple syrup.

"Why not? Whoever bought it changed his or her mind and tossed it. Think of it as recycling." Charlene began to warm to her idea. "I think it would be the perfect chance for you to go out and have a great time. Something you haven't done much of since the hurricane."

"Once we get all the repair work done, I'll start dating again. Right now, I'm too tired."

And dating wasn't all it was cracked up to be. Sam had fallen in love in college, only to have her boyfriend let her down when the accident claimed her parents' lives and injured her sister so much. He couldn't face having to deal with a paraplegic as part of his family. For a moment she remembered the crushing scene right after he visited Charlene in the hospital with Sam.

Don't go there, she warned herself. Chad was in the past. She had the future to think about. It was only once in a while that she thought about how her life would have been had that drunk not crashed into her family's car and altered all their futures.

She dated occasionally, but usually once the man found out she had a disabled sister, one who could not live on her own and would always need some assistance, he faded away. Or vanished instantly as in the case of her most recent foray into dating last August. She still had hopes of one day finding the perfect man, someone who would love her to distraction, and be able to handle having Charlene as a part of their lives.

In the meantime, Sam had other priorities. Like getting enough money to repair the kitchen and quit the nighttime job.

"I bet Margaret would let you borrow one of her gowns," Charlene said.

Sam looked at her sister. "You're not serious."

"What have I been saying? Of course I am. Think about it. The Black and White Ball is the most exclusive charity event in Atlanta. They sold out last Thanksgiving for the New Year's Eve event. It's in three days' time. You found the ticket. Think of it as serendipity. I think you should go."

"The ticket isn't mine," Sam protested. She couldn't help remembering her daydream of the previous night. She'd love to go to something so elegant. To be carefree and pretend all was right with her world.

"It'll just go to waste if you don't use it," Charlene argued. "No will know how you got it. No one would care. The charity obviously already has the money. I'll call Margaret right after breakfast."

Sam toyed with the idea. It would be wonderful to have a special memory to look back on. And when would she ever be able to spend five hundred dollars on a ticket to a dance?

Not a dance—to an elegant ball.

"Maybe—if Margaret has a dress. It has to be black or white, remember. That's the whole premise of the ball." The more Sam thought about it, the more she wondered that even if she did go, she'd be spotted for an imposter in an instant. Still—it did seem a shame to waste the ticket. Should she throw the decision to fate and leave it up to seeing if Margaret had a suitable gown?

CHAPTER ONE

SAMANTHA entered the luxurious lobby of the Atlantian Hotel with a mixture of excitement and trepidation. Her pace slowed as she looked around, taking in every detail. The spacious lobby was amazing, ceilings that soared at least twenty-five feet supporting crystal chandeliers that sparkled and gleamed with light. The floor alternated glowing hardwoods with lush Persian carpets centering seating arrangements of plush sofas and deep easy chairs. Sidestepping from a direct line to the ballroom, she deliberately walked on one of the crimson carpets, her heels sinking in dangerously. Glancing around to make sure no one was watching, she savored the luxury, smiling in sheer delight.

She felt like a schoolgirl let out into the real world for the first time. Only this was not her world. Elegant hotels, fabulous balls, expensive gowns and jewels were only things she normally read about. This was a first—to actually be participating. She couldn't believe she'd actually let Charlene talk her into attending.

Samantha assumed an air of casual sophistication and crossed to the cloakroom hoping she appeared as if she attended events like this routinely. She checked in her coat, her practical wool a poor showing beside the cashmere and silk.

Clutching her small purse and purloined ticket, Samantha

raised her chin and walked to the huge double doors opening into the ballroom. Atlanta's Black and White New Year's Eve Ball was one of the most prestigious charity events of the winter season. A recent tradition, its goal was raising funds for the Children's League while celebrating the beginning of each new year. With such sponsors as Gideon Fairchild and Vanessa Winters, it attracted the crème de la crème of Atlanta society. And tonight Sam was mingling with them all!

Samantha smiled at the white-gloved man at the door checking the coveted tickets. She showed hers wondering if he'd immediately recognize she should not be here and block her entry.

He merely glanced at the embossed ticket and said, "Table twenty-one is near the dais."

She nodded and entered the enchanted ballroom. Her gaze moved around the room taking in every lavish decoration. White lights sparkled from a dozen chandeliers reflected in the antique mirrors that lined one wall. Even more gorgeous than the ones in the lobby, the crystal illumination offered a rainbow of colors matched only by the glittering jewels displayed by guests.

Round tables were set with fine linens, bone china and real silverware. Small, discreet signs with table numbers sat in each center. Waiters circulated with champagne, filling flutes expertly. Uniformed waitresses offered hors d'oeuvres. People were already sitting at some of the tables, even more were roaming around greeting friends. Sam took her time sauntering through the lavishly appointed room. She felt like Cinderella at the ball. She didn't know anyone here, but that wouldn't dim her excitement.

People smiled at her and she returned the silent greeting with an answering smile and slight nod. Her gaze moved to the dais where a table for those sponsoring the event was already filling up. There she recognized one or two famous residents of the city from photographs in the newspaper.

True to the nature of the event, everyone wore either white

or black or a combination. The men looked superb in their dark tuxedos. Occasionally she'd spot one wearing a white dinner jacket. Young and old alike looked more polished and debonair in a tux. She wished there were more events that required formal attire. Not that she'd likely attend any of those, either.

The gowns the women wore were fantastic. The only colors were the jewels that sparkled at throats, ears and wrists. Her own string of pearls seemed subdued in comparison to the emeralds and rubies and diamonds that predominated. But they had belonged to her mother and she loved them. She could only pretend so much.

Normally when Samantha thought about white gowns, she envisioned wedding dresses. Not tonight. The creations ranged from sleek and sophisticated to almost indecent. More black gowns were present than white, but all were obviously designer creations.

Her own gown blended in perfectly. On loan from her friend Margaret who owned a vintage clothing shop, the white satin strapless bodice gradually faded into gray then black at a wide band at the bottom of the floor-length skirt. It was more than fifty years old, but had been lovingly cared for and Sam felt as comfortable in it as she would have in one of today's couture gowns. Because of its age, there was not a high likelihood of seeing another like it tonight.

She felt like a princess and held her head even higher to show off her gown. She had never worn anything so elegant before. Her hair, normally worn down or tied back in a ponytail, had been done by her sister into an upswept loop with a few curls cascading down her back. She repressed the urge to twirl around in giddy delight, feeling excited like nothing before. There would be dancing after the dinner. Would she get a chance? An assessing look around her showed most people seemed paired. Sighing softly, she made up her mind to enjoy every moment—whether she danced or not. It was unlikely she'd ever have another opportunity to attend a Black and White Ball.

"Champagne?" A waiter stepped close, a tray of filled flutes in his hand.

"Thank you," she said, taking a glass. When he'd passed on, she took a tentative sip. Mmm. Another sip. Champagne was not normally in her budget. This was delicious.

Before she could move, a man stepped in front of her.

"I'm sure we have met," he said with a grin. He sipped from his own flute of champagne and from the slight swaying on his feet she wondered how much he'd already had.

"I'm afraid not," she said with a smile.

"Fred Pearson. At your shervice." He shook his head. "Service."

He reached out and caught her arm. "Here alone? I am. Don't like to come to these events alone. Too shhhtupid, ya know? But I recognize you. I'm sure we have met."

"No. I'm Samantha." She didn't want to be rude but Fred was impeding her way to her table and she caught a couple of people looking at them. The last thing she wanted was anything to call attention to herself. What if someone questioned who she was and when she'd bought the ticket?

"I need to get to my table," she said, hoping he'd release her.

"Ah, my table is right over—" He looked around, peering at the numbers on the nearby tables, still holding on to her arm.

Sam began to wonder if it were to keep him upright.

"—somewhere," Fred ended, obviously giving up on finding his own table. "Do you want to dance?"

"The music hasn't started yet," Sam said, trying to pull away without making it too obvious.

Fred glanced around again, finishing the last of the champagne in his glass. "It'll start soon."

"I think dinner is first. It was nice to meet you. I need to get to my table."

"My table is around here somewhere," he said, stumbling a step as he turned to look around, almost pulling Sam off her feet.

"There you are. I was thinking I'd missed you."

Sam looked to her left where another man in a tux spoke to her. He looked at Fred.

"You need to let her go. I'll take over now," he said.

"Oh. Thought she was lost," Fred said, swaying a little. He looked at his hand holding Sam's arm and slowly released it. "Think I need another drink."

"I think we don't belong here," her rescuer said. A warm hand grasped her upper arm and urged her quickly to the left. Guiding her through tables and making a way through the couples standing in conversations, she was soon whisked to the sidelines.

She turned and looked properly at her rescuer—and promptly caught her breath. Her heart fluttered, her breathing stopped. He was gorgeous, tall and dark and breathtaking. He just oozed sex appeal. She'd read about that before, but never experienced it. Now she knew what the books meant. Feeling slightly light-headed, she finally remembered to breathe.

He was so tall, her head barely cleared his shoulder. Wide shoulders that gave a new meaning to wearing a tux made the suit look as if it were designed with only him in mind and the ruffles on the shirtfront served to highlight his masculinity. His hair was cut just long enough to entice a woman's fingers to thread through and dark eyes were framed by lashes a starlet would envy. His jaw was rugged. His sensuous lips curled into a slight smile, which showed a dimple indenting his left cheek. His gaze was firmly focused on her. Oh, dear, had he said something?

She blinked and looked away, her heart pounding. Good grief, she never paid attention to such things. Did coming to a ball like Cinderella give rise to Prince Charming expecta-

tions? She almost laughed, except she felt giddy with her con-
flicting emotions.

"Are you all right?" he asked. For the second time?

"I certainly didn't expect a confrontation at this ball,"
she murmured, glancing back to where Fred was making
his way through the crowd. "Do you think he'll be all
right?"

"Probably. But you never know with Boozer."

"Boozer?" she repeated.

"Fred's nickname. Rumor has it he drinks bourbon for
breakfast. He's already three sheets to the wind and he's only
just arrived. Stay clear of him."

"I shall. If I had seen him coming I would have gone the
other way. Thank you for rescuing me."

"My pleasure."

A waitress stopped by them, offering tiny crackers covered
with caviar.

Samantha hesitated. She had never tried caviar before and
had heard mixed reviews from friends who had.

Her companion had no compunctions. He took a couple,
then looked at her.

"Not having any?"

"I'll try one," she said, feeling daring. But with her small
purse and the ticket in one hand and the other holding the
champagne, she wasn't sure how.

He solved that dilemma. "May I?" he asked. He fed her
one, his fingers barely brushing her lips. She didn't even taste
the caviar, her whole being was riveted on the reaction to his
barely felt touch. She shivered slightly, but not due to cold.
She gazed up into deep brown eyes and felt her bones weaken
even as every cell seemed to stir in anticipation of more. Oh,
help, she was in trouble.

"Another?" he asked, offering a second.

She nodded and he fed her again. This time she paid attention to the strong taste by looking away.

"Mmm," she said, wrinkling her nose. She was not sure caviar would ever become a favorite.

He laughed and took another cracker for himself before the waitress moved on to the next guest.

"Not your thing, I take it," he said as he popped the hors d'oeuvre into his mouth.

Sam shook her head, her gaze on his lips as he chewed the tidbit. *Get a hold of yourself!*

"I'm glad I got to sample it. Now I know I don't have expensive tastes," she said.

"Is this your first time here?"

She nodded.

He glanced around. "Will your date know where to find you?" he asked.

"I came alone. I think Fred—Boozer—picked up on that." Did that make her sound odd? Should she make up something about her date getting sick at the last moment or something?

"So did I. If you are ready to find your table, I'll escort you," he said genially.

She smiled, suddenly feeling like anything could happen tonight. Taking another sip of her champagne, she wondered why a man who looked like he did had come alone. Maybe his date really had got sick.

"Your wife was unable to attend?" she asked, fishing for an answer without being too obvious—she hoped.

"I'm not married." His demeanor changed, instantly becoming somber.

Bad topic. She swept her arm toward the dais. "Mine is table twenty-one. The doorman said it was near the dais."

He paused for a moment, staring at her. "How interesting. That's my table also."

She went on alert. For a moment tension rose. Surely he didn't think she had deliberately set out to sit at his table? He had rescued her after all. Yet his reaction had definitely been odd. She still had the ticket out and showed it to him. He inclined his head slightly and gestured for her to walk toward the front of the large ballroom.

"My friends call me Mac," he said, placing his hand at the small of her back as they wound through groups of guests chatting and laughing with enjoyment of the evening.

"Mine call me Sam. Short for Samantha," she murmured, her heart pumping wildly—from his touch, or adrenaline, or just plain old fear of exposure, she wasn't sure. No one had challenged her so far. She should feel safe. But she couldn't help glancing around to see if anyone was paying special attention to her. Apparently not.

"Mac and Sam, sounds like a rock group or something," he responded. Twice he spoke to people as they wound through the conversing groups, but he didn't stop to introduce Sam.

The tables were set for eight. A couple was already seated at table twenty-one when Mac and Sam reached it. Everyone introduced themselves with first names as Mac seated Sam then took the chair beside her. It was obvious the others thought they had come together. She waited for him to deny it, but he ignored the assumptions.

By the time the salad was served two others had joined them. Conversation became general and Sam relaxed as the meal progressed. It looked as if her gamble had paid off. She could give herself up to the sole purpose of enjoying the evening and no longer worry about discovery. How long had it been since she'd gone out for fun and nothing more?

Longer than she cared to remember, thanks to Hurricane George.

Mac was a perfect partner for dinner. He spent his time talking with her and the woman on his other side. Two places remained empty at the table. How odd that those people had not used their tickets. Or had they, too, been trashed? The sponsors of this event had declared it to be a sellout. Was that just hype, or had something at the last moment prevented some ticket holders from attending?

When the final dinner plates had been removed and coffee served, the waitstaff quietly vanished and the night's speaker was introduced. The speech was short and poignant, urging everyone present to take up the cause of the Children's League and to be generous in support for disadvantaged children.

Then the wall to the right began to fold into panels and open revealing the dance floor and the orchestra providing the music. Along one wall a buffet table lavishly displayed desserts of all types. Two large open bars flanked the buffet tables. The rest of the room sparkled beneath the crystal chandeliers that illuminated the space, dimmed slightly to provide a sense of intimacy in the huge ballroom.

The music began and Mac turned to Sam. "Care to dance?"

She nodded, her heart kicking up again. She had hoped to have a chance, but hadn't expected such a dashing partner. As they walked to the dance floor, she noticed the covert glances given them. All for Mac, she knew. She smiled, delighted to be in the company of the best-looking man in the room.

In seconds they were on the dance floor moving to the waltz the orchestra played so well. So far so good. She'd enjoy her dance and then leave. It wasn't so awkward eating with a group but once dancing began, couples would rule the event.

As Mac continued to sweep her around the dance floor effortlessly, she forgot about the fear she'd be exposed and escorted from the ball. She could only see Mac, smell the enticing scent of his aftershave, relish the strength of the muscles beneath his jacket. He danced divinely and Samantha felt like a kid in a candy store. She loved to dance. With a sister confined to a wheelchair, however, she cherished it even more, though she rarely went to dances. Which made tonight especially delightful. Closing her eyes, she moved with the music, relishing the sensations that seeped in. Mac was an excellent partner. It had been far too long since she'd gone out for the sole purpose of enjoying herself. Perhaps it presaged a better year in the offing. She hoped so.

"You're very quiet," Mac said midway through the waltz.

"I'm enjoying myself immensely," she said with a quick glance up. His dark eyes were mesmerizing. Seconds spun by. She wanted to trace that slight dimple in his left cheek. Wanted to shift her hand from his shoulder to his neck and feel the warmth of his skin. She wanted to learn more about the stranger with whom she danced so superbly. The night was full of magic and she savored every moment. All too soon it would end and she'd be back to her day-to-day routine.

She knew she was on borrowed time, but a few stolen moments of dancing with Mac were worth any risk. If anyone official made a beeline toward her, she'd dash out of one of the doors and vanish into the night.

"There aren't many New Year's Eve parties these days that have a full ballroom and the music to go with it," Mac commented.

She nodded and murmured in agreement. She knew the ball's primary goal was to raise money, but more than anything else, it provided an elegant evening to all who attended. What a way to end the old year and usher in the new.

"Are you from Atlanta?" Mac asked.

"Born and bred," she said, giving up the quiet to respond. He was trying to talk and she was acting like a tongue-tied schoolgirl. *Get with it, Sam.* "You?"

"Born in Savannah, came here a decade ago."

"Savannah has a lot of charm. Atlanta is the New York of the South—dynamic and exciting—but perhaps it's not as charming as Savannah."

"It suits me to a T," he said.

Sam smiled and wondered what he did, where in the city he lived. What part of living here he liked best.

She wished she could say Atlanta suited her. She glanced over his shoulder, feeling the sudden aching longing for the path she once thought she'd take. Her dream of becoming a national park ranger and living in some of the western parks with wide-open spaces and nature's bounty evident everywhere had ended with the car crash that had changed her life.

Instead she was surrounded by glass and concrete and heavy traffic. And she hated almost every moment.

The music ended, but Mac kept hold of her hand.

"Since you came alone, as did I, would you care for another dance?" he asked.

"Thank you, I'd like that." She felt a tingling in her hand where his clasped hers. For a second or two she could almost imagine they were on a date together. That he was interested in her and wanted to see her again. They'd ring in the New Year together and then slip away to a quiet place just for the two of them.

But even if he asked her, she'd have to say no. Before long it would be midnight and time to leave. Even if they did spend some time together, once he met Charlene, he'd pull back like the others. The perfect man who would sweep her off her feet, loving her as no one ever had before, and committing to a life together forever, just didn't exist.

Forget commitment, she admonished herself. Until it was time to leave, she should squeeze out every last bit of fun.

When the music began again it was a faster beat. The dancing wasn't as conducive to conversation, which suited Sam. She liked dancing with Mac, but knew it was a night out of time. Monday morning she'd be back at her desk at the Beale Foundation and that night working with the cleaning crew at the towers.

When the song ended, Mac once again touched her, this time at the small of her back as he guided her from the floor. He was a sensuous man, and she felt cherished and feminine. She hadn't been touched like that in a long time and she'd never felt this way before.

"Want something to drink?" he asked, nodding toward the bar.

"As thirsty as I am right now, the only thing would be water," she said.

"Iced sparkling water it is," he said as he escorted her toward one of the large bars serving the guests. The line moved quickly. Sam watched the dancers on the floor, glancing back to the dining tables. More people were standing around talking than dancing. She would have taken advantage of the orchestra and not merely talked with friends. She didn't want to miss a beat.

"Here you go," he said, handing her a tall glass of ice and sparkling water. She drank quickly, glad for the refreshment. He'd also asked for water and finished before she did, guiding them to where a tray for empties stood. Sam drained her glass and put it down beside his.

The lights dimmed and another slow song began.

"Another dance?" he asked.

She hesitated. But temptation proved too strong.

"I'd love one more," she said.

Once they were circling the floor, Sam wondered if her imagination was playing tricks or if Mac held her even closer than before. Not that she minded. She rested her forehead against his jaw and closed her eyes again. Dancing like this was pure heaven. The shimmering feelings that swept through her only added to the magical feel of the night.

"Having fun?" he asked softly.

"The best time," she replied, realizing it was true. She was so glad she'd come.

"Me, too. More than I expected."

She pulled back and looked at him. "Why's that?"

"I thought this more of a duty event—show up, be seen, go home. You're an unexpected bonus."

She smiled. "I don't think I've ever been called a bonus before."

His phone vibrated. She could feel it as they danced.

He stopped and pulled it out, glancing at the number

calling. "Excuse me, I need to take this." He guided them to the edge of the floor as he flipped open the phone and spoke.

"Tommy? What's up? Why aren't you in bed?"

Sam watched the others dancing, but listened to the man talking. Was the call from a child?

A few moments later Mac hung up. "Sorry about that. Tommy's my son—he wanted to wait up to wish me Happy New Year, but has to go to bed now, he's too tired to stay up."

"Oh." Sam had not expected something like this. "I thought you said you weren't married," she commented, suddenly wary.

"I'm not. My wife died three years ago. Today proved to be a hard day. Our longtime housekeeper is leaving in the morning and Tommy's never known anyone else. I have a new person starting Monday, so for a few days we'll be batching it ourselves."

Sam nodded, her perception of Mac undergoing a subtle change. While he was still wildly attractive, any fantasy she might have had of them becoming a couple came to an abrupt end. She had her own baggage and couldn't see herself taking on another's. Not that children weren't delightful and a blessing, but she was already tied down. She would never achieve her dream if she became entangled with children.

"How old is he?" she asked, curious despite her resolve.

"Just three. It's a cute age."

She smiled. She wouldn't know; she didn't have the occasion to be around many young children. Her work was with disabled adults, not kids.

The music was still playing, and he took her back into his arms and they moved onto the floor once again.

It wasn't fair, Sam thought as she rested her head against him again. She wanted one fantasy evening and now that was no longer the same knowing Mac was a father and so involved with his son he'd answer a phone call in the middle of a dance.

But wouldn't she if Charlene called?

Family came first. Sighing softly, she tried to capture the sparkle from earlier. It wasn't hard being held in Mac's arms. Soon she once again pretended it was just the two of them dancing on a cloud. The music was the perfect tempo; the feelings evoked were nostalgic and warm. Unlike the experience of being held in this man's arms. She felt as if she were on the edge of a cliff—one step could send her flying, or crashing to the bottom.

When the song ended, she looked up as the countdown to the New Year began.

Ten, nine, eight…

People around the ballroom began the chant. Sam could feel Mac's arms tighten slightly as the lights dimmed even more.

…five, four, three…two…one.

Balloons popped, confetti showered down and the band began the strains to the familiar "Auld Lang Syne."

"Happy New Year, Samantha. May all your dreams come true," Mac said and kissed her.

After the first second of surprise, she relaxed. His lips were warm and seeking. She closed her eyes and relished every nanosecond. She'd met him only a few hours earlier, but it seemed entirely right to return his kiss to bring in the New Year. Her heart pounded and her body quivered in anticipation. Heat swept through her. Was this the beginning of a great year? Would she ever see him again?

He ended the kiss when the band started to play a different tune. It took a moment for her to come down to earth. Once again he led and Sam tried to get her spinning senses under control. She never did things like this. She was practical, not given to girlish dreams and foolish hopes. Still, without thought, she smiled and snuggled just a little bit closer. She felt cherished, special, connected—as if they were a couple. A woman could dream once in a while, couldn't she?

At the end of that song, the music tempo picked up and Sam pulled back. It was getting late. She should leave, however reluctantly.

"Another drink?" he asked as they walked from the dance floor.

"That would be lovely," she said. This time the line at the bar wasn't as long and in only moments they each had a glass of champagne. He touched his glass to hers.

"Make a wish," he said.

She did, for the future to be brighter than the past. Sipping, she smiled at him.

"Is that a tradition I don't know about?" she asked.

"In my family it has been. Weddings, christenings, whatever— when we serve champagne, we make wishes. Why not?"

She was charmed. If they had met in other circumstance, she would ask about his family, about other traditions they shared. But this was not her milieu. She was more the jeans-and-sweatshirt type, not one for designer clothes. Mac was perfectly at home, even speaking to people she only knew from the newspapers. Movers and shakers of Atlanta's vibrant business community.

"Shall we sit this one out?" he asked.

"You needn't spend the entire evening with me," she said reluctantly. She didn't want him to feel she was monopolizing him. And she had to leave. In a few more minutes. She'd claim just a bit more time before walking away.

"If not you, then who?"

She looked around. The only single woman she saw looked old enough to be his grandmother.

He caught her direction and laughed, leaning closer to speak softly. "She's not my type. I like pretty brunettes with chocolate-brown eyes."

Sam could scarcely breathe. He was too close. If she turned her face, her lips would brush his cheek. Suddenly she longed to kiss him again, to feel the stirring emotions his touch brought. Was he flirting with her?

She dare not take that for granted. *Remember your real life,* she admonished herself silently. Yet it seemed so far away this evening. In the normal course of events, she could never have spent five hundred dollars for a ticket to tonight's ball. She didn't move in these social circles. She was a working woman, with a dependent sister, an ancient house and no chance to change things in the near future.

He held out her chair and she sat, glad for the glass of champagne to hold on to, and to study to avoid looking at him. He couldn't read minds, could he?

"I'm sorry your wife died. That must have been awful," she said.

"It was." He sat beside her, angling his chair slightly for more room. "Chris was only twenty-eight. Who'd expect anyone to die that young?"

"That's tragic," she replied sympathetically.

"She left me with Tommy. If it weren't for him I don't know if I would have made it. But he needed me as an infant, and he needs me even more now."

The brief glimpse of Mac's personal life touched her. He appeared successful and confident with everything going for him. Who would suspect such a tragedy had befallen him?

"Hey, Mac, I didn't know you were coming. Thought you said you wouldn't make it." A couple stopped by the table and greeted him. He rose and shook hands with the man, kissing the woman on the cheek. "I changed my mind. It's a nice event, and a good cause."

The woman looked at Sam and then at Mac. "A change from your usual style?" she asked in a teasing tone.

Sam looked away. He was not *seeing her,* either. This was getting awkward. Maybe she should take this opportunity to leave, much as she hated for her special evening to end.

Another couple walked by and the first stopped them.

"Jerry, you wanted to meet Mac McAlheny, here's your chance. Mac, this is Jerry Martin, head of Windsong Industries. I'm surprised you two haven't met before."

Samantha instantly went still. Oh, no! The CEO's office of McAlheny Industries was where she'd found the ticket, crumpled in the trash. Her heart raced.

Ohmygod, she'd been dancing with the man! Talking with him. Kissing him.

She had spent the evening with Mac McAlheny!

She had to escape before he realized she'd taken the invitation from his office. She hadn't exactly stolen it—it was trash after all. But she wasn't sure the CEO of one of Atlanta's fastest-growing high-tech firms would see it that way.

She looked at the door across the room in panic. She had to leave. Right now.

"Excuse me, I need to find the ladies," she said, pushing back from the table. Her eyes met Mac's. She wanted to smile, but was afraid to do anything but escape while she had the chance. To be discovered at this late date would be beyond embarrassing.

Weaving her way through the tables and the people standing around talking, she quelled the temptation to run. She kept taking deep, slow breaths to ease the screaming panic that assailed her. Once she reached the lobby she almost broke into a run to the cloakroom. She retrieved her coat and put it on as she hurried out into the rainy night. Escape was the only thought in her mind.

The doorman called a cab and she was ushered in like royalty. She'd avoided discovery. She sighed with relief and glanced back through the rain-drenched window, but saw only the glittering lights and the doorman in his fancy uniform.

"Goodbye," she said softly. Her magical evening had ended.

CHAPTER TWO

MAC listened to Jerry talk about one of the deals he had pending all the while trying not to look around to see if Sam had returned. It seemed like a long time since she left, but it could be because he'd rather be with her than the young man going on and on so tediously about something that held no interest for Mac. His friends waited patiently for Jerry to wind down. How long could the man continue? Mac glanced back to the door. Still no sign of Samantha.

When Jerry and his wife finally moved on, Peter shook his head. "Sorry about that. He said once he'd like to meet you, but he does get enthusiastic about his work."

"Much like you do, darling," his wife said. She tilted her head slightly when Mac checked his watch and glanced at the double doors across the room.

"Where did your date go?" she asked.

Mac almost corrected her, but thought better of it. If it got back to his latest ex-girlfriend that he was seeing someone else, maybe she'd finally get the message and stop contacting him.

"Ladies' room, I believe," he said.

"She's quite different from Teresa," she said.

"Teresa and I are no longer seeing each other."

"So you've found someone new already?"

Mac took a breath. Cindy was a noted gossip. He didn't

mind her telling Teresa he was off the market, but he had no
intention of offering up Sam as a replacement.

"Let's just say I'm footloose and fancy-free."

"With no intention of getting married again," Cindy said.
"That either says marriage was hell with Chris or so beyond
marvelous you can't imagine ever duplicating it."

"You never met Chris," her husband said uneasily, as if
picking up on Mac's reaction. "She was quite a woman."

Mac felt the anguish of her death anew. Four years ago,
had they been able to afford it, Chris would have loved to
attend the Black and White Ball. But his company had only
moved into the big time after her death. He found it ironic that
she had worked as hard as he to build McAlheny Industries,
yet had died before it expanded to the successful firm it now
was.

"Well, darling, we both know Mac has so much charisma
that women naturally want his attention. And saying he will
never marry again sets up a challenge some women can't
resist."

"Or it could be that's simply the way I feel," he murmured,
wondering how rude it would be to just turn and walk away
from Cindy. He wanted to spend more time with Sam.

Cindy laughed. "So you say. You've made billions with
your business. Still—" she studied him for a moment "—I'm
telling you, women would be interested even if you were flat
broke. Something about your eyes, I think."

"I doubt it."

"So did Teresa want a ring on her finger?" Peter asked.

"Apparently. She didn't take to heart my telling her that I
wasn't marriage material. Why is it when a man's honest and
up-front, women try to change his mind? She's beautiful, but
she's not someone I want to grow old with."

Chris was the woman he'd always thought he'd grow old
with. No one could take her place. But the past couldn't be
changed. The aneurysm had caught everyone by surprise.

She'd been far too young to die. But much as he'd railed against fate, she had not lived to enjoy the fruits of their labor—or their son.

His goal now was to make a difference, for himself and Tommy. His business provided employment to more than a hundred people. He contributed lavishly to several charities, including the Children's League. Not bad for a poor kid from Savannah.

He glanced at his watch. How long did a woman need? The champagne in her glass would be warm by the time she drank it.

"Who's your date?" Peter asked.

"I just met her tonight," Mac said.

"A blind date? Oh, my," Cindy said with a laugh. "Imagine that."

"Imagine," he said dryly. He felt no obligation to explain anything to Cindy.

"Come along, darling, the music is starting again and I want to dance," Cindy said with an air kiss for Mac. "Good luck with your blind date."

As the minutes ticked by, Mac began to suspect Sam wasn't returning. He idly watched the dancing. Glancing around caused a waiter to appear with another glass of champagne. How the Children's League made money when they spent so lavishly on the ball was beyond him. But he knew donations poured in for this charity.

He looked at the table. Sam's ticket lay near the center. Was she unable to return because she didn't have it with her? He reached for it and rose. It wouldn't hurt to check to see if she was trying to convince one of the men at the door she was supposed to be here.

No sign of her when he entered the lobby. Those that had been checking tickets were no longer there. Maybe once the dinner finished, it didn't matter as much if anyone crashed the party.

He positioned himself where he could see the restroom

doors and waited. After fifteen minutes he knew Sam wasn't coming back.

He debated returning to the ball but decided he'd made an appearance, supported the charity with money. Kissed in the New Year. He could go home.

His housekeeper of several years was leaving in the morning and his little boy knew no other mother figure. Mac needed to be there for Tommy. There were two agencies searching for the right live-in housekeeper/nanny and he hoped they found someone soon. Mac didn't want his son to grow attached to Alice Horton, who started on Monday, only to break the tie with her when a more permanent arrangement could be found.

Mrs. Horton was not the solution, but a temporary fix. She had been a nanny for decades and, while sounding a bit strict, she came with impeccable references. He hoped Tommy would accept her until a new housekeeper could be found.

It was still raining when Mac gave the valet attendant his parking ticket. A good night to be home.

Or with an interesting woman who seemed dazzled by the ball yet content to simply enjoy it without flirting every moment or making sultry and suggestive comments as Teresa would have done. Samantha—Sam had made no moves on him after his impulsive kiss at midnight. Yet she'd returned his kiss with passion.

Getting behind the wheel, Mac was surprised to realize he'd enjoyed the evening. He'd gone out of duty and ended up having a good time—no, more than a good time. Sam intrigued him. That was a first. Since Chris's death, he'd made up his mind to remain single and focus on raising his son, and a chance encounter at a dance wouldn't change that. But he couldn't help thinking about Sam as he drove home. Her hair had gleamed in the light, artfully arranged and feminine. For a moment he wondered what she looked like with it in disarray, swirling around her face. Her cheeks had been tinged with color—natural, not cosmetic. But it was her chocolate-brown eyes he remembered the most. They showed her emotions, and twice he was convinced he'd seen awareness in them, as if for a few seconds she saw him as a desirable man.

Her lips had been sweet and her kiss memorable. Mac realized it had been a while since he'd felt anything when kissing someone. Teresa was beautiful, but cool and detached. Dating her had not changed his mind about wanting a new life partner. He doubted anything would.

Still, a few evenings spent together didn't mean a lifetime commitment.

Only—Sam had left with no way for him to contact her. Had it been deliberate? Had he misread the signs? He would have sworn she had enjoyed herself.

Yet she'd waited until he was occupied with Peter and Cindy and then cut out. If she'd felt any connection between them, wouldn't she have made sure he knew how to contact her?

As he pulled into his driveway, the full situation hit him. He wouldn't be going out for quite a while—not until he had a live-in nanny who would be home with Tommy. Until then, Mac had to be home each evening by six, the time Alice Horton left per their agreement when he hired her because Mrs. Horton taught an adult education class and had to be at her school by seven Monday through Thursdays.

Just as well. Dating had not played a big part of his life since Chris died and he liked spending time with his son.

But it would take a while to forget that kiss with Sam. He had tried to move on after grieving for Chris, only no one had come close to replacing her in his life. Sam was nothing like his wife, yet he could almost taste her on his lips. He remembered the warmth that had crashed through him when she'd returned the kiss. Another one or two of those wouldn't hurt. It would prove he was still living and capable of moving forward. Chris would have wanted that.

* * *

"So, how was it?" Charlene asked as soon as Sam entered the kitchen the next morning.

Sam smiled at her sister and went to pour herself some hot coffee. She'd slept later than normal because it had taken a long time to fall asleep after her magical evening. Thankfully today was a holiday, or she'd be a zombie at work. Home before one, it was actually after three before she stopped reliving every precious memory of Mac McAlheny.

"It was fabulous, how else?" she replied, turning and leaning against the counter. She glanced down at her bunny slippers, a fun Christmas offering from her sister. She sighed softly. She was much more a bunny-slipper kind of gal than elegant socialite.

"For one evening I felt like Cinderella," she said slowly.

"You looked so marvelous," her sister said.

"You told me that before I left," Sam commented, grinning. She had felt marvelous. "The hotel was fabulous. I saw lots of people who are in the newspaper all the time. The mayor was there, and our representative. The food was to die for. And I had the best dance partner in the world. Tall, dark and handsome—and he could dance better than Fred Astaire, I believe." She ended, mentioning one of Hollywood's most famous dancers she and her sister enjoyed watching in old black and white movies.

"Ooooh, do tell all!"

Sam put some bread in the toaster and began to relate every delicious memory of the previous evening to her sister. She ended with her dances with Mac.

"We danced, then I left."

"That's all?" Charlene clearly wanted more.

"Actually the tall, dark and handsome stranger turned out to be the man from whose office I got the ticket. What are the odds of that happening? Once I realized that, I left before he figured it out. I consider that a lucky break. I was worried half the evening that someone would spot me as an imposter and have me thrown out."

"You didn't do anything wrong. The ticket had been thrown away. You were just recycling," Charlene said.

"Which was the argument you used to talk me into going. And I'm glad I did, but the longer I stayed, the more chance there was of someone asking how I came to acquire a ticket."

"No one would have been so rude. And your dress fit in, didn't it? You'll have to tell Margaret all about it."

"You should have seen the designer creations there. But I held my own. It's a lovely gown and I'm so glad she trusted it to me. What if I had spilled champagne on it or, worse, caviar?"

Charlene laughed. "My sister, the champagne and caviar girl."

"Well, champagne maybe. I don't think I'll be eating caviar again." Sitting at the table, she finished her toast, still feeling the warm glow from the night before. She'd had a fabulous time. If only she could have afforded to buy a ticket on her own and gone without a care in the world. The party had ended too early for her and would never be repeated.

She'd relished the sensations she experienced wearing that shimmery satin dress. It would take a long time to forget the feelings of elegance and sophistication. A magic beginning to the New Year.

And a kiss to welcome it in. She hadn't had that in a few years, either.

She glanced up, at the coat hanging from the nail on the plywood at the back. She'd hung it on one of the nails last night to let the dampness dry.

"At least that's good for something," she muttered.

"Hey, we're warm and dry," Charlene said.

"Dry anyway. It's drafty in here. And I'm so tired of using a camping stove for cooking instead of our old gas range. It'll take weeks to finish paying off the roof before we can start saving for this repair. It's already the worst part of winter. Do we want the back wall open to the elements now? The house is hard enough to heat in winter without losing a wall for a few days." She sighed. She was back to reality with a vengeance.

Charlene gazed at the damaged space patched by panels of plywood. "It could have been worse—we could have been in here when the tree crashed through."

"We were too busy trying to stem the flood of water coming in through the attic when parts of the roof blew off," Sam reminded her. The hurricane that had freakishly blown into Georgia last September had wreaked havoc in a wide swatch of the state, including this southside of the state capital. Their roof, more than a hundred years old, had not stood up to the gale force winds. Nor had the huge old oak trees that fell beneath that force when the soil became saturated with all the water that rained down for days. Only one fallen tree had damaged the house, thank goodness. But it had done a tremendous job of taking out most of the back wall.

Insurance covered a portion of the repair costs but it was up to Sam to earn the extra money needed to finish the repairs and get their home back in order. Charlene did the best she could, but there was a limit to her work as a transcriptionist.

"Happy New Year, Sam," Charlene said, raising her mug.

Sam clinked hers against her sister's and smiled. "Happy New Year, sis."

She felt her eyes fill with tears and blinked, looking away. Only a short time ago she'd been kissed into the New Year.

"So are we going to make New Year's resolutions?" Charlene asked.

"We do each year, why should this one be different?" Sam asked, hoping her sister didn't see her distress.

"Then, I resolve to make a push to sell some of my quilts," Charlene said.

Sam laughed. "You say that every year." There was nothing

wrong with her life. She should be grateful it was as full as it was.

"This time I mean it. I'll force myself. It's not right that you have to do everything for me. I'm capable. The damage from the hurricane shows me how close to the edge we live. I need to do something to contribute to the unusual expenditure, not be a drain."

"You're not a drain. You have your job and I have mine."

"Face it, Sam. If I can get some of these quilts sold, it would help a lot and make your time working that second job shorter."

Her sister had been confined to a wheelchair since the accident nine years ago. Charlene would never walk again, nor dance, nor enjoy all the freedom that Sam took for granted. But she pulled her own weight with her home-based job and as a hobby made beautiful quilts. Some were the traditional kind that went on beds. But more and more she was doing artistic work—quilted pictures and clothing. Sam had two of her quilted vests and always received compliments when she wore them.

"And you should resolve to go back to school," Charlene said before Sam could think up a single resolution.

"I have a full-time job and am working nights until we get the house repaired. When do you suggest I consider attending classes and studying?" Sam asked. She loved the courses she took at one of the local colleges. It was taking far longer than she originally expected to get her degree, but she drew closer each year.

"I don't know, but you need to put that as a resolution. If I could sell a few quilts for enough money, we could catch up on the bills and arrange for the repairs."

"You do that and I'll look into college again." She rose and went to the sink to run water in her cup, not wanting Charlene to see how fragile her control was. She longed to return to college to finish her degree. She had less than a year's worth of classes left. Once she had her B.S., she would apply for a job with the National Park Service. She'd have to make sure she could afford living arrangements for her and her sister if she got selected. But if they could renovate this house, they could either sell it, or rent it out when they moved west. It was the only legacy their parents had left them. It was a mixed blessing, now, with the hurricane damage.

"I'll need help," Charlene said.

"With what?" Sam turned to look at her sister. She was so pretty and seemed so small tucked in that chair.

"Getting contacts. Finding someone willing to buy the quilts," Charlene said.

"Doesn't your quilting guild have contacts?"

"Not really. Everyone there dreams of selling their work for fabulous sums and becoming famous and rich. I think the patterns are a better aspect to focus on. I have quite a few I designed, you know."

Sam hadn't a clue how to market her sister's quilts. But she could find out. This was the first time Charlene had sounded like she was serious, rather than simply indulging in wishful thinking, so Sam would be as supportive as possible.

"And you should date," Charlene said. "You still have weekends."

Sam blinked at that. "What? Where did that come from?"

"You haven't gone out on a date since the hurricane. You don't have to stay home with me all the time," her sister said candidly.

"Charlene, you know I only have the weekends to catch up on chores and get some rest. Besides, I don't have anyone in mind right now. Jason at work asked me, but I don't see myself and him having anything in common except the Beale Foundation, and I don't want to talk business on a date."

Charlene bit her lip. "Well, once things turn around."

"I can't conjure up dates," Sam said, her mind instantly bringing Mac's face to the forefront. He'd be the last person she'd date. What if he found out about the ticket? How embarrassing that would be!

"But if you go places where men are, you could meet some interesting ones and get asked out."

Sam had met a very interesting man last night. Only circumstances conspired to make sure they never met again. She wasn't sure whether she wished she'd never used the ticket or not.

"Okay, the next time a presentable man asks me, I'll go out." The chances of that happening were slim to none, so she felt safe making the commitment.

"Until then, you can help me sort through my stuff and see which quilt would be the best to start marketing," Charlene said.

Mac and Tommy stood on the porch waving Louise farewell. The little boy still didn't grasp the full extent of the departure. He would begin to get it when Louise wasn't there to prepare dinner or tuck him in. And again when a new nanny arrived.

Tommy had his arm around Mac's neck and waved with his other hand. "Bye-bye," he said.

Mac waited until the car was out of sight before heading back inside. It was cold, but the rain had stopped during the night.

"Want to go to the park later?" he asked as he put Tommy down.

"Yes!" The little boy raced around in excitement. An hour or so at the park would burn off some of that energy.

Louise had left a casserole for dinner, so that left only lunch to prepare—something Mac could handle. But the next few weeks were going to see a lot of changes.

He went to his room to get his keys. He'd emptied his pockets last night, placing the contents on the dresser. Keys, billfold, tickets. Both his and Sam's. He picked them up to drop them in the trash when he noticed the numbers were sequential.

For a moment he stared at them. One was crumpled as if someone had balled it up and tossed it into the trash. From where it had been retrieved and used?

Was this the ticket he'd bought for Teresa and tossed away when he decided to break it off with her? For a long moment he stared at them, trying to come up with another scenario. How had Sam gotten hold of his discarded ticket?

Mac McAlheny arrived late at work on Monday—an unheard-of event. The new nanny had shown up on time, but Tommy had taken an instant dislike to her. Mac had stayed with his son until he had calmed down and agreed to give Mrs. Horton a chance. The woman wasn't precisely warm and loving, but was competent, as Mac knew having interviewed her twice and checked her references. She had also come highly recommended. Mac hoped she and Tommy would get along until he could sort out a more permanent solution.

"Good morning, boss," Janice said. His secretary had been with him from the beginning and knew as much about the business as he did. "Late isn't your style," she commented, following him into his corner office.

"Domestic problems, I'm afraid. Tommy didn't take to Mrs. Horton."

"Poor kid. It has to be hard on him changing like that," she said. Placing two folders on the desk, she leaned one hip against the edge. "Anything I should know before the day starts?"

They often began the day going over his appointments and reviewing updates on projects.

"Who does the cleaning of our offices?" Mac asked, glancing at the folders.

"Whoa, where did that come from?" She glanced around at the immaculate room. "Are you unhappy with the standard of work?" she asked.

"Just curious about something," Mac said. The more he

considered the idea, the more he began to think it held merit. Sam had somehow obtained the invitation he'd thrown away. The only way he could picture it was if someone from the cleaning staff had taken it. Had he or she then sold it? Or had that been Sam herself? He'd realized how little he knew about her when he tried to figure out how she'd obtained the ticket.

"The building owners arrange for that. It's in our lease they'll take care of it. If you want, I can find out who they hire."

"Please do. And then call the two employment agencies looking for a housekeeper for me and find out why there isn't one qualified woman in all of Atlanta who would like to have a live-in job keeping house and watching one small boy."

"Got it, boss." Janice headed for her desk.

Mac glanced at the phone messages, and began to return some calls. As soon as Janice had the information he needed, he'd put work on hold and track down Samantha-my-friends-call-me-Sam.

While he didn't want to think about people going through his trash, he suspected that's what had happened. Did Sam work as a cleaner? Employment these days was difficult to find, even for skilled workers.

He tossed aside the paper he was reading and leaned back in his chair. He'd been intrigued by her the entire evening. She was one of the few women under forty who hadn't tried to flirt, hadn't hinted she'd be available if he ever called. Hadn't made a big deal out of a New Year's kiss. Hadn't practically invited herself back to his place.

He remembered at the table when she'd turned from him to talk with the man on her other side. It was an unusual experience for Mac in recent years. Ever since Chris died and the company had taken off, he felt he'd become prey for determined single women. He'd shared everything with Chris— hopes, dreams, pet peeves. Now it seemed his unexpected wealth had become the most important part of his personality.

Except to Sam.

Even when he'd held her while dancing, she had not flirted. He could tell she truly enjoyed herself. Unself-consciously. Her smile had been genuine, lighting up her dark eyes. Her hair was also dark, so unlike Chris's blond mane.

He frowned. He wasn't comparing his wife with other women. There would never be anyone to take her place in his heart or his life.

The phone buzzed; it was Janice.

"Jordan Maintenance keeps this building clean," she said. "Want the number?"

"Yes." Mac jotted it down and then called the firm. In only moments, he had Samantha's last name, Duncan. The firm would not give out personal information but had let that slip. The owner, Amos Jordan, was quite flustered to have one of the building's tenants call. Mac normally would not have even mentioned the situation, but he hoped to learn more about his mystery woman. Mr. Jordan revealed nothing else and assured him the cleaning staff was of the highest caliber.

Hanging up frustrated, Mac reached for a phone book. No Samantha Duncan listed in Atlanta. Damn, how was he going to find her? Camp out tonight and wait for the cleaning staff to arrive? He couldn't do it—he had to get home for Tommy. But he'd find a way.

"But, Mr. Jordan, I didn't steal anything," Samantha tried to explain to the boss of the cleaning crew she worked for. The cleaning position, though not really a job she relished, had nonetheless been a lifesaver in providing much-needed cash with minimum training.

Now she'd been accused of theft and was being fired!

"The client was displeased. I have the reputation of my company to consider. I thought I could trust everyone, but to find someone of your caliber stooping so low is more than I care to deal with," he said.

"It was in the trash," she interjected.

"If important papers were in the trash, would you take them and sell to the highest bidder?" he asked.

"Of course not!"

"How could I trust you? If you take one thing, you could take another."

Sam rested her forehead against her palm, her elbow on her desk. Thank goodness the door to her tiny office was shut. She couldn't bear for anyone to hear this conversation.

"Please, Mr. Jordan, there was no harm done. It was trash. I was recycling," she said, giving the airy excuse Charlene had used. It was stupid. She shouldn't have done it. She wouldn't have done it if she'd been thinking clearly, but the chance for a wonderful night had proved too alluring.

And now her dream man from the ball had accused her of theft. She felt sick—not only for the accusation, but because he thought that of her. She knew she'd never run into Mac again—their worlds were light-years apart. But she wished he'd been left with a pleasant memory, not one tainted by his thinking she'd stolen something.

"I regret the situation, although I have no choice but to fire you. I will also not provide you with a reference," Mr. Jordan said heavily.

Sam took a deep breath. "I understand. Thank you for the opportunity to work for your firm," she said. She recognized the inevitable when she saw it.

"Damn," she said after hanging up the phone. She sat up and gazed out the narrow window where the sun was shining. How ironic. On the most fabulous night of her life it had been pouring rain. Now the worst thing had to happen and the sun shone.

Not the worst—that would be if Mac McAlheny made the entire situation public.

"Oh, no," she groaned quietly. She couldn't have her reputation smirched. It would jeopardize her job at the Beale Foundation.

When she thought about it, really considered it from his point of view, she could concede he had a point. Those tickets went for five hundred dollars each. Just because it had been tossed away didn't negate its value. And she'd used it as if it had been given to her.

She was stricken with remorse. It had seemed like a lark. First to find it and take it home to Charlene to show the embossed script, the fancy gold seal. Then to fantasize about attending. The actual borrowing the dress from Margaret's boutique and going now seemed like the dumbest thing she'd ever done.

Closing her eyes, she could still see Mac's eyes as he gazed down into hers as they danced. Their special kiss. Her heart rate increased thinking about it. The image dissolved as she remembered he had filed a complaint with the owner of the cleaning company.

What could she do to make amends? Send him a check to cover the cost of the ticket? And where would she get that kind of money? The entire reason she had a second job was that she was about at the end of her rope. They needed a large down payment for the carpenter to begin work on renovations to the back of the kitchen.

Charlene's salary didn't cover all her expenses, much less unexpected surprises.

Samantha's job at the Foundation didn't pay much—no job in nonprofit companies did. She'd have to find something else. Leave the work she enjoyed, the cause she embraced, for something a bit more mainstream and financially beneficial. Definitely more financially beneficial.

A job she probably wouldn't like. But she'd started at the Foundation not wanting to work for them—or in any business in Atlanta. Her dream had been so different.

But reality didn't allow for dreams. She had a house—for which she was grateful. She had her sister to care for. She had to make the most of what she had and not bemoan a future that wasn't to be.

"Double damn," she said, pounding her desk once with her fist. She had to do something—but what?

Sam fretted all morning. She didn't know if Mr. McAlheny would contact her, though Mr. Jordan had assured her he had not given out any information. But how hard would it be for a man with Mac's influence to find out her name and address? Then what?

She called home.

"Hello?" Charlene answered.

"Any calls for me?" Sam asked. She knew it was an odd request; her friends knew she worked days and called the Foundation if they really needed to get hold of her during business hours.

"Here?" Charlene asked.

"Just a thought. Don't give out my work information to anyone, okay?"

"As if I would. What's up?"

Sam debated not telling her sister, but it would come out eventually. "Mac McAlheny found out I used his ticket and called my boss at the cleaning service. I was fired."

"What? Why?"

"For indiscretion," Sam said softly. She still couldn't believe it.

"So if he threw away a fan and you fished it out of the trash, that would be a problem? That doesn't make sense. We were recycling. People do it all the time. Throwing something away ends ownership."

"I guess a case could be made for that," Sam said. "But Mr. Jordan didn't see it that way."

"So now what?"

"I look for another job and hope Mr. McAlheny doesn't come breathing down my neck."

"Gosh, sis, I'm sorry. I know I urged you to use the ticket. I never expected you to lose a job over it. Can I do anything?"

"Pray I can find another part-time job soon."

The rest of the day Sam alternated from nervousness every time her phone rang, to panic about where she would find a second job to help pay off their debt.

Just before leaving that evening her boss popped his head in through her open door.

"You remember the business luncheon tomorrow, right? I'm hoping my speech will loosen some wallets. I want you and Pam there to handle any donations we may get."

Sam nodded. "I've had it on my calendar for weeks, ever since you told me, Tim. We'll both be there from eleven-thirty on. Maybe some of the guests will take a brochure or something prior to lunch and offer a few thousand dollars on the spot."

"That's always a hope."

Raising funds for worthy charities was getting more difficult. There were so many deserving organizations, but with companies tightening their belts to make sure their bottom lines continued to be robust, available corporate donations were drying up. Sam's boss, Timothy Parsons, had been scheduled to speak at this luncheon for weeks.

Sam liked attending events like this since it gave her an opportunity to discuss the wonderful work of their Foundation with people who may not know about it. While not her first choice of professions, her work at the Foundation was important to her.

Nothing untoward had happened the rest of the day. Anonymity should prove enough protection—she hoped.

That evening shortly after dinner was finished, Sam studied the want ads in the paper. Most were for day jobs or required specialized training. It was depressing how few jobs there were that she could do, and even more so how few part-time jobs. Nothing popped out at her.

Charlene was in her studio, as they called the former dining-room-turned-quilting-haven. Her sister was so talented in that area maybe Sam should look at marketing the quilts until another part-time job appeared. It would be wonderful if Charlene could overcome her shyness and sensitivity to being in a wheelchair and sell some of the lovely works she'd created. Not only for the much-needed income, but as a boost to her sister's self-esteem.

How did one go about marketing quilts besides visiting specialty shops and seeing if the owners would take them on?

The worry that she hadn't heard the last of the purloined ticket nagged at her. If Mac wanted to make an issue of her using the ticket, she'd pay him the cost of it. She wasn't sure how she'd come up with the money on short notice, but there had to be some way. She tried to think of something of value they owned that she could sell.

Charlene rolled her chair into the kitchen. She took out some juice and went to the lower cabinets where they stored dishes. Glancing at Sam, she frowned. "No luck?"

"Huh? No, none. How's the vest coming?"

"Just about finished. Then I want to bind the wall hanging of the garden scene."

It was common for the women in Charlene's quilting guild to donate some of their work to the annual Beale Foundation Boutique that the Foundation hosted each December. All proceeds went to the Foundation. Sam privately thought her sister's work the best of the bunch, but Charlene received none of the money her creations brought in. If only she could find a steady buyer for her work. The garden scene she referred to was a picture quilt and Sam thought it was stunning.

But she knew better than to expect some fairy godmother to show up out of the blue to buy all Charlene's quilts.

"Want to rent a movie for Friday night?" Sam asked, folding the newspaper and putting it aside.

"I'm going to Betty's for dinner and to see her new quilt. She used my pattern and I want to see how someone else interpreted it. She's picking me up at six. I forgot you won't be working nights anymore. Want to join us? I'm sure she wouldn't mind," Charlene said.

"I'll pass." It wasn't often her sister went out. When Sam had worked for Jordan Cleaning, her evenings were full. Now she had a break. For a moment she wondered if it would be too late to enroll in spring classes at the local college.

No, she was being stupid to even consider it. She had to find something to supplement her income to afford their repairs. Maybe she could find another evening job this week and be busy again by Friday. She went back to studying the ads.

CHAPTER THREE

WHEN Sam entered the large restaurant, which hosted the business luncheon, she was immediately surrounded by people she knew. Caroline Bentley's law firm donated regularly to the Beale Foundation. She was accompanied by one of her law partners, Ted Henley. Then Sam greeted two CEOs of companies who also routinely gave funds to the Foundation. She enjoyed catching up on snippets of news as she worked her way to the table assigned her. Her counterpart, Pam, and their boss, Tim, were sitting at separate tables, so between the three of them they could speak to more guests.

There were twenty tables of eight set up. A nice turnout, Sam thought as she took a chair with her back to the lectern. She already knew what Tim had to say; this way she could judge reactions while he talked.

Things settled down shortly after noon when everyone took a chair and the meal began. As the waiter was placing the salad in front of Samantha, she looked up—straight into the eyes of Mac McAlheny!

He sat at the next table over, in her direct line of sight. He lifted one eyebrow at her, but could not do more across the distance.

Flustered, Samantha looked at her plate. Good grief, what was he doing here? She peeked again to see him still watching her. She hadn't a clue he'd be one of today's guests. Would he cause a scene? She couldn't tell anything from his expression and she wasn't sure she wanted to find out. Could she somehow find an excuse to leave? He didn't know she worked for the Beale Foundation. Maybe he'd think she was the CEO of some firm he didn't know. All he knew was she once worked for Jordan Maintenance.

The man at her left spoke and she gratefully grasped the diversion. She made a special effort to engage each person at her table, giving information about the Foundation in practical terms, resisting the temptation to look over at the other table again. But it was an effort and she felt her nerves on edge the whole time. Mac was watching her. Some sixth sense made that clear. How far would he go in a public forum like this? She didn't want to put it to the test.

When Tim was introduced, some people shifted their chairs slightly for a better view of the keynote speaker. She risked a glance at the other table. Mac's gaze was narrowed and focused directly on her. She shifted slightly so she wasn't in his line of sight. Listening to Tim with only partial attention, she glanced around for the nearest exit. When the luncheon finished, people would be leaving, chatting, creating a barrier between her and Mac. She could zip out through the exit on the side before Mac confronted her.

Samantha was ready to make her move as soon as Tim finished. She quietly gathered her purse and tote that carried pamphlets for the Foundation. She'd already distributed most of them before lunch. The applause was heartfelt and she was pleased Tim's speech had gone over so well. But now—

"I must admit his speech pushed me over the top," the man next to her said. "I'd like to discuss a donation. I like the idea of a perpetual gift, one that keeps generating income over the years. If our own fortunes continue to increase, we could add to the gift each year. And if not, the Foundation would still get income from the initial grant in the name of our company. Are you the lady I talk to?"

Samantha sighed softly. No escape.

Smiling brightly, she put down her purse and tote. "I sure am, Mr. Hadden. And the Beale Foundation would be grateful for any donation, but a gift that keeps giving is especially appreciated." She dug into her tote for the proper pamphlet explaining gifts-that-keep-giving and handed it to him. "As you can see, you have a choice of ways to do this. I can run some numbers if you give me an indication of how much you wish to donate."

Her body went on alert. Without turning, she knew Mac stood right behind her. She longed to turn and glare at him for disturbing her peace through lunch. Maybe if she continued to talk with Mr. Hadden, Mac would get tired and give up.

Ha, who was she kidding? She knew CEO types; they were focused and persistent. Ruthless, some said. A man didn't build a company being easily dissuaded.

"I'll have to talk to my chief financial officer, but I was thinking something along one or two million to begin with. This is a good year for us. I like the way your Foundation works," he said.

Two million dollars was a huge donation. Samantha had to keep talking. Would Mac please, please, please leave?

"In addition to accepting donations, we'd also like to encourage businesses to hire people with disabilities. There are many tasks that are easily handled by people with some limitations. I know a deaf woman who works with data entry and analysis. She's a whiz at it. Another young man who has strong computer skills is working in an electronic engineering firm. He's been working for only a few months and has already received a promotion because of his excellent work. One older woman in a wheelchair is perfect at customer service. She is on the phone all day and has improved the company's image of customer caring. She received a bonus at Christmas that almost equaled her annual salary. Please, give some of our registered prospects a chance," she said.

Sam handed Mr. Hadden three more pamphlets. "Many people don't look beyond the obvious disabilities to the true talents of people who are slightly different."

"I'll have my HR people look into that as well," he said.

"I'll take a couple of those brochures," said one of the other CEOs at her table who had been listening.

She thanked them all and then, unable to put it off, gathered her things and rose. Please don't let him make a scene here in front of potential donors, she prayed, scrambling around for an excuse that would get her off the hook.

A warm hand lightly grasped her arm and turned her gently. Not unlike the other night. But this time she wasn't moving away from danger, but directly into it.

"Hello, Samantha Duncan," Mac said.

His voice sounded as warm as honey on a summer's day. A quick glance up at his face assured her she'd not forgotten a single thing about him. His dark eyes were just as compelling. That slight dimple in his left cheek called to her. She still ached to trace the indentation, feel the texture of his skin. Fisting her hands to resist, she forced a smile.

"Hi." Her heart pounded. Her skin felt too tight. People chatted as they made a general exodus from the restaurant. The waitstaff was clearing tables and moving some of the furnishings to reconfigure for their normal seating. She felt caught like a fly in amber.

"I listened to your brief discourse about the Beale Foundation. Have you worked there long?" he asked.

She could hardly concentrate, with his hand holding her and her worry he'd accuse her of theft. The delightful sensations that swept through her made her want to lay down her purse and put her arms around him. Would he kiss her as he had on New Year's Eve? Or threaten her with the police? Was stolen property valued at five hundred dollars a cause for misdemeanor or felony?

Get a grip, she admonished herself. He was not going to

have her arrested. At least she hoped not. If he wanted to, he would have already taken action. She tried to quell her rioting nerves with that rationale.

"More than eight years," she said, hoping the trepidation didn't show.

"Interesting," he said.

"Perhaps your firm would like to give a donation or hire a partially disabled person," she said brightly, trying to ease her arm from his grip. His fingers tightened slightly.

"It went well, don't you think?" Timothy Parsons said as he strode over to join Samantha. Pam came over and both looked expectantly at Mac.

Samantha wanted to sink through the floor, disappear and never have to face any of them again. She gave in to the inevitable.

"Timothy, I'd like you to meet Mr. McAlheny. This is my boss, Timothy Parsons, and my coworker, Pam Barnnette."

"Good to meet you," Tim said, reaching out to shake hands. Mac was forced to release Sam's arm in order to return Tim's greeting. She sidestepped out of reach and stood halfway behind Pam, resisting the temptation to turn and run for her life.

"I'm impressed by the work your Foundation does. I was hoping to get some time with Samantha to discuss it further," Mac said smoothly.

"Excellent. Carry on. I'll see you back at the office," Tim said to Sam. In only seconds he and Pam left her alone with Mac.

Traitors. Only they didn't know how much she did not wish to be left alone with Mac McAlheny.

Once the others were out of earshot, she glared at him. "If you really wish to discuss the Beale Foundation, Tim would have been a better choice. He's the head of our Ways and Means Division."

"After eight years on the job, I expect you know as much

as he does. Which raises the question, what is an accomplished businesswoman like you doing cleaning offices?"

He was going to challenge her on the ticket. At least he'd waited until they were virtually alone. She didn't count the busboys moving about their tasks.

"I need the money."

"Ah, to fund an extravagant lifestyle," he said smoothly.

"Hardly," she returned with a short laugh. "To fund the consequences of Hurricane George."

She caught the change in his attitude. His mocking ceased and he looked almost thoughtful. Yeah, right, like that was going to happen. Men like Mac never had to count pennies or worry about how to make needed repairs. She'd bet Hurricane George hadn't dented his place, much less caused major damage which exceeded his ability to repair.

"So maybe you can tell me more about the Beale Foundation over dinner," he said.

She blinked at the unexpected comment. Turning, she began walking toward the exit. "If you really want to discuss contributions, I'd be happy to do so, but I suspect that was just a ploy to get rid of my boss." She took a deep breath. "I know what you really want."

"Oh?" Mac felt a kick of amusement. He'd been stunned when he looked up from the luncheon program and found himself staring at Sam. He normally did not believe in coincidence. When he wanted something, he usually had to work to get it. He'd had no luck in finding out more about Samantha than her last name and had begun randomly calling a number of the Duncans listed in the Atlanta phone book to no avail. With a bit more patience, he could have saved himself a lot of trouble.

He refused to closely delve into the reason he'd gone to such lengths to find her. Here she was, of all places. It hadn't made sense at the onset.

He'd watched her during the entire time he ate. She looked

polished and professional and seemed to relate well to the people sitting at her table. Twice she'd glanced his way. Once she reminded him of a doe caught by headlights—she'd looked downright stricken. The other glance had been more surreptitious, as if verifying he was still there.

Once the after-lunch speech finished, he made directly for his quarry and been impressed with her discussing huge grants with Hadden. He knew the man only by reputation, but she'd handled him perfectly.

"So what do I really want?" he asked after a few seconds of silence. Tension seemed to radiate from her. He leaned a bit closer to better hear her.

"Retribution for taking the ticket. It was in the trash, you know," she added quickly.

"Retribution? It was indeed in the trash. I bought it for someone, then ended that relationship. Having no further need of it, I tossed it. I haven't a clue what you mean by retribution."

"For me to pay for it or something," she muttered, picking up her pace. They reached the doors to the outdoors and Samantha sailed through, stopping short when a gust of cool wind blew right in their faces.

"I'll get a cab," he said, gesturing for one as it approached.

Before she could argue, he ushered her into the vehicle and climbed in beside her. She scooted to the far side, probably wishing the space was larger.

"Where to?" the driver asked.

Mac looked at her.

She gave the driver an address and then threw Mac a wary glance. Was there some hidden message in that?

He studied her for a moment. She apparently thought he was out for some kind of payback for the ticket. Was that all that was keeping her from at least being somewhat glad to see him? He frowned. He didn't care if she were glad to see him or not.

He almost laughed, for the situation was proving farcical.

For the past three years every time he turned around another woman was waiting to pounce. Now he'd found someone who rebuffed his every move. Cindy would have to revise her estimate that Mac had charisma after all.

"I can't pay back the ticket at this time," she said primly.

"Forget the damn ticket," he said. "It's not important."

"After you got me fired over it? I don't think so!" Sam retorted indignantly.

"*Fired?* What are you talking about?"

"Didn't you call Mr. Jordan and accuse me of stealing the ticket?"

"Of course not. That is, I called him, but only to find out who you were. I hoped to find out some way to locate you. I realized eventually that you weren't coming back to the table on New Year's Eve. Your ticket was still on the table and it was the next one issued after mine. I put two and two together and tried the cleaning service. How else would you have suggested I find out how to contact you?"

"Well, Mr. Jordan took it wrong, because he fired me Monday morning, and I really needed that job."

"Cleaning offices? I thought you worked for the Beale Foundation."

"I do, but the pay is not the greatest. After George ripped off the roof of the house and caved in the back with a huge oak that crashed in under the force of the wind, money has become more important."

"Didn't you have insurance?" he asked, surprised to hear the reason she had to take a second job.

"Only partially. I didn't know I was supposed to update it periodically as property values rose. So it covered some, but not the full amount."

"Hence the second job?"

"Which I no longer have, thanks to you," she said, flaring at him.

"That was *not* my intent."

"Gee, that's good to know. You got me fired all the same."

"So come to dinner with me and donate the savings in your food bill to the house fund," he said whimsically.

"What?" She stared at him.

Mac watched her expression. There was something about Samantha Duncan that intrigued him. How many women did he know would take a second job to pay for something without whining or looking for sympathy? Or even a handout once they realized he had money to burn.

"Why did you want to find me?" she asked, her eyes narrowing as she gazed at him.

"To see you again. Come to dinner Friday."

"Since I probably would have had a sandwich on Friday night, I'm not sure the sixty cents or so it would save me to eat with you will help a lot," she said.

He was hard-pressed not to laugh. "I'll double the savings."

"This is all a joke to you, isn't it?" She glared at him.

"No. Have dinner with me and we can discuss ways for you to get that money you need for repairs."

She glanced around as the cab slowed. They had reached their destination.

Mac didn't know why it was important she agree to see him, but it was.

"So you'll have dinner with me Friday?" he pushed.

She shrugged. "Why not. It's not like I have a job to get to anymore."

Mac had had more enthusiastic responses to budget meetings, but he'd take what he could get.

"I'll pick you up at seven," he said.

"I'll meet you at the restaurant," she countered instantly. "I don't know you, Mr. McAlheny. I prefer to keep meetings in a public place and keep my home life separate."

The cab swooped into the curb in front of the small office building that served as headquarters for the Beale Foundation.

"Thank you for the ride," she said, lifting her tote and handbag.

"Francesca's on Monteith Street, seven o'clock," he said, getting out and assisting her to the sidewalk. "And it's Mac, remember?"

"I'll be there," she said and turned without another word to enter the building.

Mac watched her for a moment. As he entered the cab, giving the driver the address for McAlheny Industries, he considered how dating Samantha would be different from seeing Teresa. Samantha Duncan was unlike any other woman he'd met. She didn't seem impressed with him or his company. In fact, she was downright mad at him. How was he to know a simple inquiry would result in her dismissal?

She was as unlike Chris as anyone he'd known—not that it mattered in the long run. He wasn't looking for a relationship that lasted for any duration. He had a business to run and a son to raise.

For a few weeks, maybe they could share some good times together.

Was he getting jaded? Date one woman for a short time then move on?

Yet what choice did he have? He was not planning to have his heart ripped out again by falling in love and having it end abruptly through death. Life was chancy enough without putting himself in situations that could hold him hostage to fate.

By Friday afternoon, Sam was a nervous wreck. She had not come up with an excuse to avoid dinner with Mac. Maybe something would happen to make the engagement impossible. She tried to quell the escalating kickboxing butterflies by repeating it was only a meal with a prospective donor to the Foundation. The discarded ticket had been discussed and he'd surprised her by inviting her to a meal rather than threatening her with the police.

On the other hand, if he hadn't talked to Mr. Jordan, she would be working tonight and not going to dinner at one of the best Italian restaurants in Atlanta.

A dusting of snow had covered the city yesterday and some traces lingered in spots. When Sam left the office, night had fallen and the glittering streetlights reflected on the patches of snow, glistening white in the dark. She found a parking place just a block away and entered the restaurant promptly at seven. She immediately spotted Mac leaning casually against one of the walls in the lobby, watching the door. He pushed away when he saw her and walked over. The butterflies increased their activity. She drew in a deep breath. She could handle this.

"Hi," she said, suddenly feeling shy.

"Hi yourself," he said. "Want to check in your coat?"

"Yes." She slipped out of it before he could help her and handed it to him. This wasn't the Black and White Ball. She needed to keep her wits about her. He stepped to the cloakroom and checked it in. He tucked the ticket in his pocket. No escape that way tonight, she thought.

"Our table's ready, I told them you would be here at seven," he said, guiding her into the large dining room. The maître d' greeted them both and led them to a small table near the far wall. Most of the tables were already occupied. A large Reserved sign sat in the center of theirs, which was swiftly whisked away.

"How did you know I'd be on time?" she asked when seated.

"You're the type."

"What type?" She glanced at the menu, her mouth watering at the selection. His words caught her by surprise.

"Competent, businesslike, not someone to waste time—your own or someone else's," he said while also studying the menu.

Sam wondered if she liked the assessment. It sounded

boring and dull. Which she probably was. Who had time to develop exciting traits with all her responsibilities?

When she looked up, his gaze was fastened on her.

"What?" she asked.

"I wasn't sure you'd come," he said.

"You told my boss you wanted to discuss the Foundation. Besides, this beats a tuna sandwich."

Knowing he wasn't as certain about her joining him made her feel better about the evening. Despite his wealth and standing in the city, he had human doubts just like she did. She tried to keep that thought in the forefront of her mind.

They began discussing the Foundation's goals and the question came up about how Samantha had started work there.

"So Charlene is the real reason I'm there today," she finished, after giving him a brief recap of the car crash that had killed her parents and rendered her sister paralyzed from the waist down.

"A lot of responsibility for one so young. You must have been only about twenty-one when it all fell on you," he said.

"Actually I was nineteen. I had to quit college and find work fast. We were lucky in one way, however. The house had mortgage insurance and upon my dad's death, was paid in full. So housing is one expense we don't have to worry about."

"But you worry about others?"

She shook her head. "We're not here to listen to my woes. Are you going to donate to the Foundation or not?"

"Persistent, aren't you? Yes, McAlheny Industries will give a perpetual gift, like Hadden."

His cell rang. Checking the number, he frowned. "Excuse me," he said, answering the call.

From his side of the conversation, Samantha could tell it was from a babysitter. She remembered Mac had spoken to his son at the ball. She couldn't hear the other end of the conversation, but it was obvious the little boy wasn't happy about his dad being gone. Mac talked to him for a few minutes, ending with, "I'll see you in the morning as soon as you wake up, okay?"

He replaced the phone in his pocket. "Sorry about that."

"That's okay," Sam said.

"Do you remember I told you at the ball that we just lost our longtime housekeeper and nanny? Well, Tommy doesn't like the new one I've hired. She's daily and only agreed to stay longer tonight as a special favor. I need a live-in nanny fast and so far none of the agencies I've contacted can locate a suitable one." He looked at her again.

"What?"

"After we spoke the other day, I called Jordan Maintenance and spoke again with Amos Jordan. You're right, it's my fault you lost that job. I have one to offer you in exchange."

Sam just looked at him. Instead of making an issue of the ticket, he was offering her a job? What was he up to?

"I'm listening," she said after a moment.

"I'm looking for a live-in housekeeper—"

"I'm not interested." Good grief, live with the man? She'd never get any sleep. She was having enough trouble these nights dreaming about their dances, that special kiss. How could she possibly consider working for him?

"Hear me out. I have a woman coming in from seven in the morning until six at night. But she leaves promptly at six, unless we make prior arrangements like this evening. I can't get away from work at a set time every night. I need someone to watch Tommy from six until I get home."

Sam nodded, feeling a spark of anticipation. "So you're offering me a babysitting position until you hire a live-in nanny?"

"Seems the least I can do to make up for your job loss." He mentioned a sum above what she had been earning at the cleaning service.

"How late do you work?" she asked. Jordan had paid her for six hours of work each night.

"Sometimes as late as ten or eleven. Most nights I try to get home before Tommy goes to bed at eight."

"Hourly rate?" she asked.

"Flat fee per week, some nights you may be there until almost midnight. Most nights you can leave before eight."

If most nights proved true, she'd be receiving more than she received before for only two hours of work each day. How hard could it be to watch a three-year-old for two hours?

She was undecided. Wary of a deal that sounded too good to be true, she was tempted by the income. And fewer hours would mean she could work with her sister to devise and implement firm plans for marketing Charlene's work this year.

But to work for Mac McAlheny? She wasn't sure that was wise. He affected her on a primal level. Could she work for him and not want something more?

"I've never worked with children before. Surely you could find someone else better suited."

"Come meet Tommy, see what you think," Mac said.

Sam considered the offer. It sounded perfect. If things would once go her way, she could get the repairs finished and paid for and resume her night school college work. She was so close to her degree and eventually the career she longed for. That's what she had to do, keep her eye on her goal and not get sidetracked by a gorgeous man looking for help with his child.

Sam hesitated a moment, then nodded. "Okay, I'll meet your son and see where we go from there."

Mac smiled with satisfaction. He would get to see more of Samantha Duncan—and find out exactly why she caught his interest. The current situation was perfect for hiring her. It would atone for causing her to lose her job and help him out after Mrs. Horton's rather strict rules. He had an idea Sam would be good for Tommy. And, perhaps, for him?

CHAPTER FOUR

SAMANTHA drove home thoughtfully. She wasn't sure if she understood why Mac McAlheny had offered her a job. She tried to analyze it from all different angles. She didn't think he was angry she'd taken the trashed ticket. In fact, he seemed content to talk about a variety of subjects at dinner—including a perpetual grant for the Beale Foundation.

But his job offer had come totally out of the blue. Why had he made it?

She'd never worked with small children. Could she be what Tommy McAlheny needed? For the most part they would only spend a few hours together before the little boy went to bed at eight. How hard could that be? Then she'd just need to be there until Mac returned.

But what about weekends? He'd mentioned he'd need her to watch his son occasionally on the weekends when he had to travel or work on a special project. He had not said anything about watching his son while he dated—but Sam knew that would be part of it. She frowned when she thought about him taking someone out for dinner and dancing. She couldn't possibly consider him *hers,* but even she knew that New Year's Eve kiss had been special. Even now, several days later driving a car through the dark streets, she could almost feel the sensations that had zinged through her with his kiss.

"This is strictly a job," she said aloud as if to dispel the memory.

Charlene was not home when Sam arrived. It was unlike her sister to be out so late. Sam hoped it meant she was having fun at her friend's house. Normally Charlene invited friends to their home, which was set up for wheelchair access to everything on the first floor. It was hard for her to get in and out of cars and maneuver in other homes that weren't wheelchair friendly.

Sam changed into her warm nightgown, donned her robe and slippers and went down to fix some hot chocolate. She was just about to go upstairs when her sister returned so she veered to the front of the house to greet her.

"Hi," Charlene said, turning in the doorway to wave at a departing car. She closed the door on the cold and spun around to face Sam.

"You must have had fun…you're so late getting back," Sam said with a smile.

"We had a ball. Talked and compared notes on quilting. She showed me what she'd done using my pattern. It turned out great. How was dinner?" she asked as she pulled her jacket off.

"I'm not sure. I went thinking we would be talking about the Foundation, but I got an offer of a different kind. I may end up watching a small child for a few hours each evening."

"How did that come up? I didn't know you knew anything about taking care of kids," Charlene said.

Sam took her sister's jacket and hung it on the lower of the closet poles and picked up her chocolate she'd placed on the small entry table. "Want some hot chocolate?"

"No, I'm full from Betty's meal. Spill."

"It's not a sure thing yet—I'm to meet the little boy tomorrow. If we hit it off, I'd start Monday after work. It's still an evening job, but when else can I find a second job?"

"Should beat cleaning offices for six hours a night.

Maybe you can rock him so you sit for a while," Charlene said with a smile.

Sam sipped her beverage. "I'm not sure three-year-olds like to be rocked. That's more for babies. We'll see. He may not like me." Then what would Mac do?

"I was heading for bed." She wanted to think about their dinner and the commitment she'd made.

"Me, too. I had fun tonight, but I'm tired. Good night, sis."

Sam climbed the stairs to her bedroom as Charlene headed down the hall to hers. She hadn't told Charlene all the details and wondered why. Perhaps because she wasn't sure about the job. Yet despite the uncertainty, she felt a spark of excitement.

She'd get to see Mac again. Get to learn a bit about his personal life and meet his son. The child he'd had with his wife. Was he over her death yet? Did he keep her pictures around for this son to see?

And what all would he expect of his son's nanny? Could she live up to his expectations?

She sure hoped so.

Mac lay in bed. The dark was complete except for the faint spray of stars he could see from one of the windows. It was late and he should be asleep. But he was thinking.

Mrs. Horton was competent, but more old-fashioned and strict with schedules. Tommy seemed to be subdued around her. When Mac questioned her about their evening, she'd said only that Tommy had gone to bed right on time. As if she'd allow anything else.

Would his son like Sam?

What was there about her that had him making such a ludicrous job offer out of the blue? She'd been worried about the blasted ticket—afraid he'd be upset she'd used it. He considered her finding it an act of providence. Now he'd wanted a way to see her again.

In a few weeks, hopefully sooner, he'd find the perfect live-in housekeeper and not need for Sam to babysit Tommy.

But until then, he'd see her almost every day. Surely in a short time he'd grow indifferent to her and move on?

He turned his head slightly, not able to see in the dark the photograph of Chris that sat on his bedside table, but knowing it was there. She was laughing, the delight of her happiness shone through in that candid shot. He missed her so much. But it was becoming harder and harder to feel her with him. Her laughter had enchanted him yet its echoes had long ago faded. Her blue eyes would forever live on in Tommy. But tonight, instead of seeing her, he saw Samantha Duncan. Her face danced in his mind anytime he closed his eyes.

He hoped he hadn't made a mistake hiring Samantha. But when he'd heard about the damage the hurricane had done, and realized his call had gotten her fired, it was the first thing that came to mind as a way to help. She might go after funds for the Beale Foundation, but Sam wasn't one to take charity herself.

Mac threw off the covers and grabbed a shirt to pull on over the shorts he slept in. He wasn't getting any sleep thinking about Sam. Maybe he'd put in a few hours catching up with e-mail. She'd be here tomorrow and he couldn't wait to see her in his home.

The next morning Samantha dressed in warm jeans and a thick cable-knit white sweater. She had debated for a while about what to wear to meet Tommy. Hearing the echo of her mother's voice, *start as you mean to go on,* she eventually just wore what she was comfortable in. She'd probably be down on the floor playing with the little boy; no sense wearing dress slacks for that. Be yourself, was another axiom from her mother. People will either like you for who you are or not. But you'll never have to worry they are your friends only because you are acting like someone you are not.

She was not some glamorous socialite who traveled in exalted circles in Atlanta. She was a working woman who had a dream to move west. It might be an impossible dream, but it was all hers.

Charlene had prepared waffles for breakfast, with warmed maple syrup and spicy sausages. Sam headed for the coffee first, however.

"Looks great," she said as she sat down.

"I heard you moving around so knew how to time the meal," her sister said as she rolled into her place at the table. "So what time do you go?"

"Ten o'clock. I think if I hit it off with the little boy, I'll stay for a bit while his father is there, so Tommy can get to know me. The longtime housekeeper they had left last week and Tommy isn't so fond of the new nanny. She leaves at six each evening, so I'll just have time to get there immediately after work."

Charlene looked at her. "Where's the mother?"

"She died when the little boy was a baby."

"How sad. Goodness, she couldn't have been very old. I hope you get the job, sis. You'll be perfect at it. Look what good care you take of me."

Sam shook her head. "You make it easy for me. And you could sell those beautiful creations you make to bring in money. We really have to do something about marketing them this year."

Charlene nodded, not looking as confident as she had on New Year's Day.

Sam felt the edgy nervousness increase as she drove to Mac's home. She wanted to make a good impression on the little boy and had stopped at a toy store to buy him a picture book. She didn't know if it was in order to bring a present. Would Mac think she was trying to bribe his son into liking her?

He'd be right.

Vacillating from wishing to clinch the job to panic at taking care of a small child only added to her nervous state. One way or the other, she'd soon know if she had the position.

She studied the house when she turned into the driveway. It was large, built of stone, with soaring peaked roofs and a huge front lawn. From the treetops she could glimpse behind the garage, the backyard was probably even larger. Still, for the home of one of Atlanta's richest men, the house wasn't that opulent.

In two minutes she knocked on the door, rubbing her palms against her jeans, trying to quell the jitters.

Mac opened the door and for a moment she forgot to breathe. He'd been gorgeous in a tuxedo. Looked sophisticated and dynamic in a business suit, but wearing casual attire had her heart beating even faster. From the navy crewneck sweater to the dark cords and black boots, he oozed sex appeal. Maybe this had been a mistake. His eyes drew her attention. They were dark and deep and so intriguing. She wished she was coming for an entirely different reason.

"Good morning," she said. Her voice sounded rusty and she cleared her throat.

"Right on time," he said, opening the door wider so she could enter.

A small boy stood on the stairs, staring at her with wide eyes. He ran down the last few steps to his father, encircling one leg and peering around at Sam.

She smiled at him but kept her distance. "Hello, you must be Tommy. I'm Sam."

"Sam-I-am?" he said, quoting from *Green Eggs and Ham* by Dr. Seuss.

"No, not that Sam. I know your daddy and he said you needed someone to come watch you after your nanny goes home each day."

"When Mrs. Horton leaves and before I come home, Sam will stay with you. Remember I explained that?" Mac said, reaching down to pick up his son. The two males turned to look at Sam. Tommy studied her gravely.

"I brought you a present," she said, offering the wrapped book.

"You didn't need to do that," Mac said. He looked at Tommy. "What do you say?"

"Thank you." He gave a big grin and reached for the package.

Sam's heart about melted. The little boy had the same dimple in the same place as his father. His blue eyes were unexpected with his daddy's dark ones. His mother must have given him those eyes. She wondered if his mother had been a blonde as Tommy had a head full of blond curls. She glanced at Mac. He was Tommy's father…she could see the strong resemblance—except for the coloring.

"You are very welcome," she said in response to Tommy's thanks. "I hope you like it and that you don't already have it."

Mac took Sam's jacket and hung it in the closet, all the while juggling Tommy and the big book.

"Let's go into the family room. Tommy's toys are there," Mac said, leading the way down the hall.

Sam glanced into the large living room as they passed—a huge fireplace dominated the far wall with windows flanking it. The furnishings looked oversize and comfortable. Still, it was lovely. Far more spacious than the living room in the house she and Charlene owned. When she entered the family room, Sam was pleasantly surprised by how homey it looked. Kid friendly, yet designed with adults in mind as well. There was a breakfast nook between it and the open kitchen.

"This is beautiful," she said, putting down her purse and sitting on the edge of one of the sofas.

Mac sat on the one at a right angle to the one she sat on and put Tommy on his feet. In only seconds the wrapping paper had been torn off and he showed the book to his dad.

"Something to read later," Mac said. "Thank you."

"Wanna see my truck?" Tommy asked Sam.

"Yes." She watched as he ran halfway across the room and picked up a large toy truck and raced back to her, offering it for her inspection. It set the tone for the day. He was an open and friendly little boy whom Sam thought she could manage for a few hours every evening.

Mac leaned back on the sofa and watched as Sam and his son grew acquainted. He'd wondered all last night what he'd been thinking when he asked her to watch Tommy. He wasn't so impulsive as a rule. He had inquiries out at two leading employment agencies in town, yet had hired a virtual stranger to watch his son with no background check, no references. Only his gut feelings.

Not that Mrs. Horton wasn't a stranger—but she'd come with loads of references. He knew next to nothing about Samantha Duncan except that he was attracted to her. Looking at Sam had him thinking about kisses and dancing cheek to cheek and even lazy evenings watching a television movie complete with fire in the fireplace and shared popcorn.

Whoa—where had that fantasy come from? She was trying out for the role of his part-time nanny, not his lover.

He rose suddenly and they both looked at him in surprise.

"I just remembered something I need to do. I'll be back in a little while." He waited for a moment in case Tommy didn't want him to go, but when his son turned back to Sam, he left. Entering his home study a moment later, he closed the door and glared at the picture of Chris on the credenza. "Why did you have to die and leave us?" he asked. It was a question he'd asked often over the years. "It makes life so much more difficult," he said.

But her sunny smile did not seem to take in the difficulties he faced. She would forever be happy and beautiful and young. He'd have to find his way alone.

"It's not like I'm going to fall in love again," he explained as he walked over to her picture and picked it up. "It's just chemistry. She's pretty, I'm lonely. It's nothing like what we had." They'd shared dreams together, worked together to build a marriage and a business. When their son had been born—for a few brief hours they'd thought they had it all. But she had died before she could leave the hospital after Tommy's birth. At least he had the comfort of knowing everything had been done to try to save her. He would have forever wondered about that if she'd died at home.

Mac studied the picture for a long time. In the back of his mind he knew he was running scared. Chris would not have wanted him to be lonely. She'd loved life and embraced it fully. She'd probably whomp him on the arm and say, *go after what you want.*

But her death had crushed something inside him. Trust. An ability to believe in the future. Work gave him an escape and when he concentrated on the problems and challenges of building McAlheny Industries, he felt alive. When faced with the loneliness of the nights in bed, he felt half dead. Only his son kept him from devoting all his time to work.

"You would have adored our son," he said softly to the picture, setting it gently back on the credenza and turning to see what he could do for a little while, giving Tommy time to get to know Sam at his own pace. He hoped he was doing the right thing hiring Sam.

For a moment, he wondered if it were the right thing for Tommy, or for himself.

After Tommy finished explaining the truck and all it could do, in which Sam understood about one word in three, he picked up the new book and said, "Read me?"

"Sure thing." This she could handle.

He handed her the book and then lifted his arms. Sam pulled him into her lap and opened to the first page. In only a moment they began a new story about Thomas the Tank Engine. She'd bought it in honor of Mac's Tommy.

Sam was surprised at how easily the child accepted her. Was it because he knew his father was home? Or would they be able to spend their evenings harmoniously, too? She hoped so. He leaned trustingly against her as she read. Sam had never read children's books to kids before. She was two years younger than Charlene. Had her sister read to her? She didn't remember.

The story was soon finished and Tommy asked for it again. Amused, Sam complied. By the fourth time he asked, she asked him if he had other stories, or wanted to play a game.

He struggled off her lap and went to the cupboard near the fireplace. Opening it, he took out three books and ran back, offering them to Sam.

The morning passed swiftly. Once in a while Sam wondered what Mac was doing, but she was enchanted with Tommy and had fun keeping up with him.

"Can we go to the park?" he asked.

"Is there a park nearby?"

He nodded and ran to the front of the house, opening the closet door. "Jacket."

Sam followed, wondering where Mac was and if she should be taking Tommy out into the cold.

Mac had obviously heard them and stepped out of a room opposite the living room.

"Going somewhere?"

"I wondered where you were. Tommy wants to go to the park. Is that something he does?"

"We go frequently on the weekends when the weather's nice. I'll go with you, show you where it is. If you work on a Saturday, you'll want to go to the park and let him run. It burns off some of that energy. And then he'll take a long nap to boot."

"Ah, tricks of the trade," she said, glad for any hints she could get.

The walk to the park took five minutes. Sam paid strict attention to the way in case she did bring Tommy on her own. Mac kept hold of his son's hand and would not let him run on the sidewalk, though Tommy asked several times. Once they reached the grassy area near the playground, Mac let him go and the little boy ran straight for the slide.

"He's adorable," she said as they followed more slowly. There were other children and parents at the park. Benches were placed on the perimeter of the playground in locations that gave good access to the various play structures. The slide Tommy ran for was a curved one. Sam saw three other slides of various sizes, in addition to swings, seesaws, balance beams and a fort with cargo netting on one side and a fire pole on the other. There was even a suspension bridge between two platforms.

"He won't fall, will he?" she asked, already a bit wary of the relative height of the slide in comparison to the small child.

"He's played on it many times. If he does fall, we'll just hope he doesn't get hurt."

"I wouldn't want him to fall," she protested.

"I don't, either. But I'm not going to coddle him and deny him a chance to explore his own boundaries. This park is safe. The mulch beneath the playground equipment is several inches thick, cushioning any falls. It scared me to death the first few times we came, but I'm getting better," he said with a wry grin.

Sam felt her insides melt at his look. She nodded and turned back to watch Tommy. She wasn't so sure she should take this job. Anytime she was around Mac she wanted to be the center of his attention. She relished the special feelings she experienced when he looked at her. His grin turned her upside down. He made her feel things she'd never felt before.

Not that anything could come of it. She had her sister to consider. In the past anytime a man got interested in her, he'd meet Charlene, take one look at the wheelchair and soon thereafter vanish from her life. Charlene hated it, knowing she was the cause. Sam hadn't felt a tremendous loss at any time since Chad. That had been hard to take. She had truly been in love and thought he had been as well.

But she was more concerned for her sister than for any man so shallow he'd let something like that influence his life. How could she risk her sister's feelings again? Besides, Mac had never given her an indication of any interest beyond caring for Tommy.

Except the kiss at the beginning of the New Year.

And dinner last night.

This wasn't a date. It was a job interview.

"Tell me what he can and can't do so I don't panic if we come on our own," she said, keeping her gaze and attention firmly on Tommy McAlheny. There was no return to day-dreaming about his father.

By the time Sam left it was after one. Upon returning to the McAlheny household, Mac has shown her where things were located in the kitchen. She and Tommy had explored his bedroom and Mac had explained some routines Tommy followed. A lunch of peanut butter and jelly sandwiches and milk had been shared and Sam had actually tucked the little boy in for his nap.

She turned into her own driveway satisfied she'd quelled any personal thoughts about Mac and could handle the task of watching his son until they had enough money to pay off the roof and get the back of the house repaired.

Charlene was in her quilting room, putting the finishing touches on the wall hanging she'd been working on. "I guess from how long you were gone that the job is yours?" she asked as soon as Sam entered.

"It is and Tommy is darling. I wish you could see him. He has blond curls and big blue eyes. He talks a mile a minute, but I miss some of the words. I hope this works out. The money is good and the job is so much better than working for Jordan Cleaning." She was not going to tell Charlene any of her mixed feelings about working for Mac. She was not even going to think about Mac for the next—three seconds. She sighed. She had to get over this obsession.

"What are you working on?" Sam turned the topic of conversation to her sister's work and soon they were discussing ways of getting it into the hands of boutique owners who might be interested in carrying some of her quilts.

"I could just go door-to-door," Sam mused as she fingered the pretty vest her sister had just made. "If I wear this, the owners are sure to be interested."

"Sounds too easy. There are women in my quilting guild who have tried that. Too many great quilts, too few outlets."

"But they are trying to sell bed quilts which don't compare with the art pieces or the clothing you've made. And you have your patterns. Have you tried a fabric shop to see if the owner would offer them?"

Charlene shook her head. "I'll think about it."

"How about the place that you buy all your material from?"

"Why would someone want my patterns?"

"Why would they not? The designs are fantastic. Think how many woman love to quilt but aren't creative enough to come up with special designs."

Sam wondered who she might talk with to find out more about marketing. She was a whiz at fund-raising. How much different would this be?

She wondered if Mac's marketing team would have any suggestions. Could she find a way to ask? After she'd proved herself taking care of Tommy, of course.

Monday evening promptly at six, Samantha knocked on the door at Mac's home. An older woman answered a moment later.

"You're Ms. Duncan?" she asked.

"Yes, call me Sam. Are you Mrs. Horton?"

The woman opened the door wider and stood aside so Sam could enter.

"I am. Glad to see you're prompt. I hope that continues. I have class to get to."

"I will always do my best," Sam said, a bit surprised by the less than friendly greeting.

"I'll be off. The boy's in the family room watching Mickey Mouse."

Sam took off her coat and hung it in the closet, setting her purse on the entry table. She took a deep breath and headed for the family room, glad Mac had given her a tour of the house on Saturday. Mrs. Horton didn't seem like she wanted to stay a moment longer than she had to.

"Hi, Tommy," Sam said.

He looked up and his expression lightened. He launched himself off the sofa and ran to Sam. "Hi." He lifted his arms and Sam reached down to scoop him up, hugging him. "How are you?" she asked, smiling at his sweet face.

"I watching Mickey Mouse," he said, turning to point to the television.

"So I see. Shall we watch it together?" she asked.

A moment later they were sitting on the sofa, Tommy in her lap, watching the Disney character.

"I'm off, then," Mrs. Horton said, coming into the kitchen. "There's a casserole in the oven, which will be ready by 6:30. I hope you'll clean up after you eat."

"Of course," Sam said. She would not get upset by the woman's austere attitude, but secretly wondered how she interacted with Tommy all day.

"Bye, Tommy," Mrs. Horton said.

"Bye," he said, waving, his attention on the television.

When the show ended, Sam switched off the television and went to prepare their meal. She set Tommy on the counter so he could help, making sure she was never more than a step away.

The little boy looked enchanted. She handed him a spoon and he held it carefully. Taking down two plates, she took the hot casserole from the oven, placing it on the counter across the stove from Tommy. There was crusty bread on the counter which she figured was also for dinner.

"I helping," Tommy said proudly.

"You are." She handed him the bread. "Hold that until I'm ready to cut it, okay?"

"'Kay," he said, solemnly holding the bread.

The back door opened and Mac walked in.

She looked up in surprise. "I didn't expect you home so early," she said.

"Daddy! I helping," Tommy said proudly, clutching the bread to his chest.

"So I see." Mac came into the kitchen and gave his son a kiss. He looked at Sam. "I thought I'd see how things went this first evening. It looks as if you have everything under control. Is there enough food for me, too?"

The casserole would feed a family of six. "Plenty. Do you need me to stay?" If he were home, he had no need of a sitter for Tommy.

"Please. I'll be working in the office part of the evening. Just wanted to make sure you found everything you needed. Mrs. Horton left at six, I take it."

Sam nodded, hoping that was the reason and not that he didn't trust her. She took down a third plate and carried it to the table. Taking the bread from Tommy, she lifted him to the floor. "Here," she said, handing him two forks to go with his spoon. "You set the table. Put these on the table and come back for napkins."

Tommy was clearly delighted to be put to work. Mac leaned against the counter and watched.

When they sat at the table, the settings left lots to be desired, but Tommy was clearly proud of his contribution.

"Good job," Mac complimented him.

Sam nodded again and began to serve the plates, giving Tommy a small portion.

"He won't eat all that," Mac said when she put the dish down on the table.

"Too much?"

"He's only three. He doesn't eat a lot."

"I'll remember that. She served his plate and then hers. Tommy squirmed and ate a few bites, talking to his father, telling him something fascinating, Sam thought. But once again when he began these long monologues, she didn't understand most of the words.

Mac began to laugh. Sam watched him, intrigued by the change. He should do that more often. His eyes crinkled in laughter and his whole face seemed younger. That enticing dimple appeared and she knew she was staring. He caught her gaze and shook his head.

"I don't understand half of what he says, but he's so earnest about it."

She smiled and looked at Tommy. For a second she thought of how they'd look to an outsider peering in. This was like a normal family. Father, mother, child. The kind of dinners she remembered when her parents had been alive and she and Charlene the much-loved children.

Feeling a pang at the loss of her parents, gone nine years, she shook off the feeling and rose to get Tommy some more milk. He might not eat much, but he loved milk.

Sam felt on edge as the meal progressed. Was she on probation? Every time she looked up, Mac was watching her. He'd look at Tommy or at his food when she caught his eye, but it made her nervous. If he hadn't thought she capable of watching his son, why hire her?

Once finished, Mac rose. "I'll be in the study if you need me. Have Tommy come see me before he goes to bed."

She breathed a sigh of relief when he left. She had Tommy help clear the table carrying things that couldn't break if he dropped them. Quickly cleaning the kitchen, she checked the time. Almost seven-thirty. She'd give Tommy a bath and read him a book before having him say good-night to his dad.

Leaving the door a bit open after she'd tucked Tommy into bed, she went quietly to the stairs. Mentally running through her checklist, she had done all she was supposed to. She waited a moment at the top of the stairs to make sure Tommy wasn't calling out, then went down. Mac waited near the bottom.

"In bed?"

"Went quietly. I always thought kids protested," she said, slowing as she descended the last couple of steps.

"He's always been good about going to bed. I wanted him to get used to your tucking him in. Normally if I'm home, I do it," he said. "He seems taken with you."

"I'm glad. He's so darling. It doesn't feel like work to watch him."

"He's not always so congenial. Sometimes he throws temper tantrums like any kid."

"And when that happens, do I just ignore them?"

"For the most part. Do what you feel is best."

It didn't sound as if he didn't trust her. She frowned. "So why did you come home early?"

Mac didn't answer for a moment. Then shrugged. "Just to make sure you didn't feel thrown in over your head your first night."

"Can you hear him in your study if he cries?" she asked.

"Yes, I have a baby monitor there. And another in the family room. So nights you're here after he goes to bed, you can hear him if he cries out. Though he rarely gets out of bed in the night."

"Okay. Well, I've cleaned the kitchen to Mrs. Horton's standards, I hope. Tommy's in bed, so I'll be off," she said, stepping away. She wished she could stay and talk, find out more about Mac and what he'd done all day. Share some of the surprising contributions that came in after last week's luncheon. But he made no move to detain her.

"I'll be home late tomorrow night," Mac said.

"I'll be here until you arrive," she replied, going for her coat.

"Drive carefully. It's getting colder, so there may be some ice on the road." He took a step closer and took her coat from her hands. Her gaze met his and Sam felt the butterflies again. She needed to develop some kind of immunity to the attraction that flared every time she was with him. She was hired to watch his son—nothing more.

Slowly she turned around and let him help her put the coat on. When she turned back, she met his eyes again. They were dark and mysterious and compelling. She could look at him forever, if she could only breathe at the same time.

Taking a quick breath, she broke off the eye contact. "Good night, Mac." She had to get out of here before she did something stupid.

He opened the door for her. The way he watched her made her conscious of how she must look after a long day at the office and then taking care of his son. No lipstick. And who knew how her hair looked?

"Good night, Sam."

What she wished for, she thought as she turned on her car engine a moment later, was a kiss, not a polite good-night.

How stupid was that? Mac didn't seem the type to play around with his staff. The kiss at New Year's had been magical, because of the setting, the nostalgia at the end of a year and the promise of a new one. And probably loneliness because he missed his wife.

"Well, that puts me in my place," she said as she carefully backed out of the driveway and headed for home. "Cinderella was a fairy tale. Not my life."

Mac stood in the doorway watching Sam drive away until the cold had him step back and shut the door. He listened for a moment, but heard nothing. Tommy was already asleep.

Returning to the study, he sat behind the desk and leaned back in the chair.

He'd done some checking on Samantha Duncan—from one of her biggest fans, Timothy Parsons at the Beale Foundation. He was full of praise for Samantha's work and the fact she'd overcome obstacles at a young age that would have defeated older women.

Mac learned more about the accident that had changed the direction of her life. And about her sister, Charlene, whom Timothy also held in high regard.

Taking the ticket had been a lark, Mac was sure. It sounded unlike the woman he was coming to know. He had thrown it away after all. Was it fate to put her into his path? he wondered. He'd enjoyed dinner tonight more than any dinner recently— except perhaps the one on New Year's Eve. Louise had always had dinner ready when he came home but she refused to eat with them. Tonight he had not given Sam the choice. He had some prior commitments the rest of the week, but he'd see what he could do to be home for dinner in the future.

Tommy seemed to like her.

Mac was pleased, since he knew Mrs. Horton and his son didn't hit it off as well. At least for a few hours a day, his son would have someone he really liked to be with. Mac had called the agencies again this morning, but there were no prospective live-in housekeepers on the horizon. He'd expanded his search with two more agencies. Surely someone was out there who would relate well with Tommy, and keep his house.

Not that he was in that much of a hurry now. It would mean he'd have to let Sam go. He was looking forward to some more dinners together before then.

By Friday, Sam felt she was in a comfortable routine. She left work to head for Mac's house. She and Mrs. Horton would never be best friends, but the woman was considerably more cordial now than on Monday. Tommy loved seeing her arrive and she was surprised at how much she relished his enthusiastic greetings.

And she took a few moments before leaving each evening to speak with Mac about what Tommy had said or done. He had not returned home before Tommy's bedtime after Monday. Still, he was always eager to hear about his son. He'd also ask how Sam was faring and listen as if truly interested.

Tonight she wondered if he was taking some lovely young woman out for dinner and dancing. The weather continued cold but clear. Tomorrow it was forecast to warm up a bit, at least above the freezing mark. Mac had asked her Wednesday night if she could watch Tommy on Saturday and she'd agreed. Maybe she'd take him to the zoo. She remembered loving to visit the zoo as a child. She'd have to get Mac's permission tonight. Wouldn't that be a nice surprise for Tommy if his dad agreed?

She had a hard time thinking of Mac as anyone's father. He seemed too sexy to be connected with children. She considered the Black and White Ball the perfect setting for Mac. Or as head of a large corporation. Yet he obviously adored his son and Tommy loved him equally.

She had never given much thought to marriage and a family. Since Chad had broken her heart, she'd been determined to get her degree and go after the job in the National Park Service she so wanted. She so longed to see the west, to live in a national park where land was as it had been for millennia. Some nights she could hardly stand her life the longing was so strong. She read books, had several travel videos of the western parks. She knew more than the average person on flora and fauna of the western region. Maybe once she had a job, she'd find just the right man. Maybe another park ranger.

One day she'd get her chance. But being patient was hard.

Not that she regretted providing a home for her sister. But if Charlene could find an outlet for her quilts and become totally self-sufficient, that would free up her sense of responsibility a bit. Once Sam had her degree, everything would change. Nothing would stop her from her goal.

Sam drove through Atlanta's evening traffic heading for Mac's home. She forced her thoughts to the job at hand and not the dreams that had languished for years. Anticipation rose. Even though he was probably escorting some other woman to dinner, she'd see Mac when he returned home. Those few moments at the end of each evening caused Sam to check her makeup, replenish lipstick and brush her hair as soon as Tommy went to bed each night.

It wasn't much, but for a few moments each day, she relished being in Mac's company.

CHAPTER FIVE

AFTER Tommy was in bed, Samantha brought out the book she'd been reading and settled in the large recliner in the family room. Glancing around, she relished the peace and quiet. Tommy had been more rambunctious this evening than normal and she was glad he was finally asleep.

Mrs. Horton kept the house immaculate and Sam was grateful for the serene room to relax in. This job sure beat working for Jordan's. She could feel guilty for taking Mac's money for the few hours she'd worked so far, but he'd made the offer and she really needed the supplemental income.

The book held her interest until fatigue won out. She'd worked long hours all week and the quietness of the house soon lulled her to sleep.

Mac pulled around Sam's car and into the garage. It was late. He hadn't meant to stay at the party so long, but Peter and Cindy were there. While Mac never liked Cindy all that much, he and Peter had been friends for years. For a little while it had almost been like old times—he talking with a friend while Chris had been elsewhere at a party talking with her friends. Only he knew the difference. They would not be going home together.

To his surprise, he'd enjoyed the evening.

Entering the family room, he saw immediately that his

babysitter had fallen asleep in the recliner. He closed the door quietly, hoping he hadn't wakened her. For a moment he studied Sam, her hair tousled and mussed. Her long, slightly curved lashes brushed the top of her cheeks. Her lips were devoid of lipstick, but still looked kissable.

He frowned and shrugged out of his coat, slinging it across the back of the sofa. He hadn't forgotten their kiss at the ball. She'd been receptive, but that was before he knew her or she him. Would she be equally receptive tonight? The past week he'd found it difficult not to rush home every night to see Sam. When he did arrive, she properly gave him a rundown of Tommy's activities and then quickly left.

He'd offered her the job because he'd gotten her fired and believed in righting wrongs. But now he wanted more than a mere employee. He wanted someone to talk to, someone who cared a bit for his son and his best interests. He wanted something beyond what he'd shared with his former house-keeper, Louise.

But would Sam ever want the same thing? She'd been so proper and distant this week. An employee-employer barrier? Or was she really not interested and that was her way of showing it?

There was only one way to find out. He crossed to the chair and brushed her hair away from her face. The gentle touch seemed to waken her. She blinked once and then looked up at him.

"Sorry, I think I fell asleep." Her voice was husky. She looked warm and content and alluring.

"No problem, as long as it was after Tommy did."

She nodded and stretched, pushing her breasts against her sweater.

Mac swallowed hard. He sat on the armrest, reining in on the impulse to pull her into his arms and snuggle together in the warm chair. "Busy day?"

"Busy week. I'll get my stuff and head out," she said. But

before she could rise, he stood and offered her his hand, pulling her to her feet.

"Thanks," she said.

She tugged on her hand, but he didn't release it. Looking up, she raised her eyebrows in silent question.

Slowly he rubbed his thumb across the back of her hand. "Thanks for watching my son. I'm glad you came into our lives."

Sam looked as if she didn't know what to say. After a couple of seconds, she smiled wryly. "Maybe it was meant. If you hadn't thrown away the ticket and if it hadn't fluttered out of the trash, we never would have met."

He didn't want to think their meeting was so chancy. He would have met her at the charity luncheon. But would he have? They'd sat at different tables. Normally when he went to such events, he left as soon as the program ended.

"Come to dinner tomorrow night," he said, giving into one impulse.

"I can't," she said. "I need to spend some time with my sister. I've been here every evening all week."

"Bring your sister." It wasn't his initial thought, but he'd be glad to include her if it meant Sam would be back.

She shook her head then looked thoughtful. "You and Tommy could come to our place," she offered slowly.

That surprised Mac. But he'd take what he could get. "Fine. What time?"

"Actually, since you wanted me to watch Tommy tomorrow, I was going to ask if I could take him to the zoo. They have a great petting zoo. I think he'd love that. Then I could bring him back to our place and you come over when you are finished or by six or so. Would that work?"

He nodded.

He still held her hand. She tugged again and he let her go. She was instantly all business—giving him a report on Tommy and then going to get her coat. He helped her put it on, turning her to face him, his hands on her shoulders.

"Thanks for taking such good care of my son this week," he said.

"It's a pleasure. He's so funny and sweet. He cuddles up like he's known me all his life. You have a great son."

He nodded, watching her lips as she spoke. When she stopped, he kissed her. He felt her start of surprise and then the giving as she returned the kiss. He gathered her close, unwittingly noticing she was smaller than Chris. Her mouth was warm and sweet and the taste of her sent waves of pleasure through him. All thought of Chris fled. This was Samantha of the pretty brown eyes and the taste of sunshine.

He wanted her in his bed.

But would they ever reach that stage?

Sam ended the kiss a moment later by turning her head slightly. She was breathing hard and her mouth was rosy and damp from their embrace.

"I need to go," she said, avoiding his eyes.

He turned her face and tilted it up until she met his gaze.

"Thank you again for all your help with Tommy." Should he apologize for kissing her? He didn't regret a second.

She stepped back. "It's my job, isn't it?" With that, she opened the door and hurried into the cold.

With a start of surprise, Mac realized he wanted it to be more than that.

"Stupid, stupid, stupid!" Sam chanted as she backed out of the driveway and began driving home. She needed to keep her distance. Was she sending some kind of vibes that she was fascinated by him? Was that the reason he kissed her? Of course she was totally fascinated, but she worked hard all week to keep that knowledge under wraps. She hardly spoke about her job or Mac to her sister. She kept her second job a secret at work. No one could accuse her of flirting. She didn't linger when he returned home each night, though she longed to settle in the comfy sofa and share a late-night beverage of coffee or hot chocolate and talk. She wanted to find out all she could about the man and what he thought about current issues. What were his future plans? Was he as much fun at the end of a hard day at work as he was when on a date?

But she'd been determined to keep her distance.

So why had he kissed her tonight?

She swerved the car slightly as she let herself delve into the memory of the kiss. It had been better than the one at New Year's. At the ball, at least, there had been some excuse. Tonight she was at a loss to know why. Yet she couldn't help the slight smile that touched her lips. Who cared why? Apart from the ball, she hadn't been kissed in a long time. And never like Mac kissed.

Oh, no. She'd invited him to her home. Now she was going to introduce him and Tommy to her sister, share a meal together in her home—which couldn't begin to compare with the lavish place in which he lived—and have to make small talk without revealing how his touch affected her. Or giving away her confusion to her sister.

Not that she wasn't content with her own home. How many women her age owned a house that had no mortgage? Most of the rooms were fine—it was the kitchen that needed work. And a little touch-up here and there from the water damage when their roof leaked.

She groaned. How in the world was she going to cook an impressive meal using camping burners and no oven? What had she been *thinking?*

She hadn't been, obviously. Still, she was excited to see him again. And tomorrow evening she wouldn't feel like Tommy's nanny, but a competent woman entertaining at her home.

What would Charlene say?

She had acted instinctively—not wanting to miss a chance to spend time with him but knowing she should spend time with her sister after being gone so much.

What a mess. Now she had to explain everything to Charlene, without giving away her mixed-up feelings. Then spend the day at the zoo with a three-year-old and still come up with some kind of meal to impress Mac.

Panic set in. Taking a deep breath, she tried to calm herself. She didn't have to impress him. She could cook spaghetti, that didn't need an oven—except for the garlic bread. Maybe she could use her neighbor's oven for that. Ruth had been generous in offering her kitchen whenever the Duncan women needed it. They'd taken her up on it a couple of times.

There, one problem solved.

Now if it were just as easy to explain to Charlene…

Timothy Parsons had been to dinner a couple of times. Now she was inviting her new boss. It sounded weak when she considered she didn't feel the same about having Mac over compared to Timothy.

And after only a week? The reasons for the invitation she dared not reveal. She wanted to see him again when she wasn't strictly Tommy's nanny. Was that a rational reason? Would Charlene see through it and suspect the truth? That Sam was fast getting a crush on her new boss?

And if she did, so what?

Sam could admit she admired Mac. But that's as far as she could go. She had her own plans for the future once she could swing things financially. And right now that did not include being tied down to Atlanta or the obligations Mac would bring to a relationship.

It was merely a friendly dinner for her boss. She needed to keep that thought firmly in mind.

Sam dressed warmly the next morning. The temperature hovered around freezing. She debated canceling the zoo visit, but really thought the little boy would love the exhibits. They'd visit the petting zoo and then stop for some hot chocolate to warm up before returning home. Even though it had been years since she'd been to the zoo, she remembered vividly the many outings her parents had taken Charlene and her on. They'd been such fun. She hoped to make it as fun for Tommy.

When she arrived at the McAlheny home, Mac met her at the door, dressed casually. Was this how he went to work on Saturdays? She let her gaze roam briefly from the wide shoulders down the long legs, and felt that nagging increase in her heart rate. She took a breath and stepped in, smiling widely, hoping he couldn't see how he affected her. Just because she was intrigued with the man didn't mean she had to show it to everyone—especially not him!

"It's freezing. Tommy needs to dress warmly," she said as she stepped inside. Trying to ignore the attraction she felt around Mac could prove a full-time effort in itself. She longed to reach out and touch his arm, just to connect. He had looked fabulous in his tux, dynamic in his business suit, but now he was so downright sexy that if he kissed her this morning, she'd be a goner.

She looked around for Tommy. The sooner they left, the better for her. Nothing like a shock of cold air to erase any lingering longings.

"He's dressed as warmly as I could get him. Cords, wool socks and he even has mittens that Louise knit for him," Mac said. The little boy came running into the foyer, his face alight. He ran up to Sam and hugged her legs.

"Are we going to the zoo now?" he asked, leaning back and lifting his arms for her to pick him up. He wasn't the lightest thing, but she relished the sturdy little body in her arms and happily picked him up for a hug.

"We sure are. I see you're dressed for cold weather. It's sunny, so I think we'll be okay. And after we see the animals, we'll stop for hot chocolate."

"Yeah! I love hot chocolate," he said, beaming. Then he squirmed to get down. "Let's go, Sam."

* * *

"Jacket and mittens first," Mac said. He patiently put the jacket on his wiggling son. Handing him the mittens, he watched to see if Tommy could manage on his own. With a glance at Sam, he said casually, "I thought I'd join you if you don't mind. My meeting today was canceled." No need to tell her he'd been the one to cancel it. Somehow compared with seeing his son enjoy a visit to the zoo, the meeting on production planning came in a very distant second.

She looked at him in surprise—that wasn't horror on her face, was it? If so, she recovered swiftly.

"Oh, well, then if you can take him, I needn't go." He definitely picked up on the disappointment in her voice.

"He's been counting on you," Mac said, knowing that would ensure her going. He felt he was getting to know Samantha Duncan and how her mind worked.

"Oh." She bit her bottom lip for a moment. He wanted to reach out and brush it with his thumb, feel the soft warmth against his fingertips. Feel her against him again like last night.

"Okay, then we'll all go," she said as if making up her mind.

He hid his amusement as he went to get his own jacket. Sam should never play poker; she didn't hide her feelings very well. She clearly didn't want him along, but wasn't willing to disappoint Tommy. It was easier to have two watch Tommy than just one as she'd find out once they were at the zoo. He planned to enjoy himself and he hoped she did, too.

Mac insisted on driving since the car seat was already in place in his car. Tommy talked nonstop about seeing monkeys and petting animals and drinking hot chocolate. At least that was the gist of his excited discourse. Mac was glad Tommy didn't feel the undercurrents swirling around in the car. It seemed as if Sam had gone tongue-tied on him. She gazed out the window, her hands clenched into fists. Every time he glanced her way he noted something new. Her profile was pretty. Nice nose, classic lines, soft hair pulled back so it wouldn't fly into her face with the breeze.

Everything about her was pretty and feminine—from her dark hair to the faint pink tinge on her cheek. Her skin looked soft as satin and he knew her lips were. Swallowing hard, Mac forced himself to focus on the road and driving in the light traffic rather than keep looking at his son's nanny.

He refused to think about the kisses they'd shared, that would likely have them ending up in a crash. He'd save up those memories for nights when he felt especially lonely in his bed.

The zoo was not crowded even though it was a Saturday. Probably because of the cold weather. The wind was light, but really carried a bite. They entered through the Flamingo Plaza, the birds not in evidence. He hoped they were bundled into someplace warm. Tropical animals wouldn't fare as well in today's cold spell. Only a few hundred yards from the parking lot and he already wanted out of the cold.

Sam reached up and undid her ponytail, allowing her hair to cover her ears and neck hoping for some warmth. She suspected this outing had been a mistake. It was freezing! She held Tommy's mittened hand and wished she'd brought gloves. How long before they could stop in one of the restaurants and get warm?

"Maybe we should stop for hot chocolate before venturing to the petting zoo," she said as she watched Mac zip his jacket closed.

"I don't think all our party would concur," he murmured.

Tommy was pulling Sam along as he charged ahead, his excited voice talking about animals and petting. His exhilaration was contagious and she felt her own spirits lift in response.

"Okay, we'll see the petting animals then go somewhere warm."

Once in the children's zoo, she let go Tommy's hand and watched him run a bit ahead.

"My hand is cold after holding his," she said, smiling as the little boy skipped and ran to see the giant tortoise. Before she could think, Mac took her hand in his warm one.

"Can't have you getting frostbite. You may need to drive home," he said, tucking both hands in his jacket pocket.

Cold fled. Warmth swept through. A moment later she could speak. "Why is that?"

"Because I may freeze to death before it's time to go. Your hand can keep me warm, too." He looked down at her and she was struck again by how gorgeous the man was. Holding hands meant she was right beside him, feeling the warmth from his body along hers. She wanted to lean closer, find a sheltered spot out of the cold and just gaze at him forever.

However, duty called and she dragged her gaze away to look for Tommy. He was talking to another little boy next to the giant tortoise. She wondered if the other child could understand him any better.

"I should have checked the long-range forecast before offering this treat," she said as they followed Tommy when he darted here and there to see everything. They reached the petting area and entered, finding it marginally warmer with all the small animals crowding around. It was also sheltered from the wind.

Tommy was in heaven. He solemnly followed the instructions of the zookeepers on duty and gently patted the rabbits and the goats. There was a donkey. A cow. And ducklings and baby chicks in a warming box.

Sam enjoyed the little boy's reaction to all the animals. His laughter rang out when one of the baby pygmy goats gently butted his side. But she was totally caught up in the feelings racing through her holding Mac's hand. She struggled against releasing all the cares of the world for a short time. She wanted him to pull her into his arms and kiss her until she forgot about the cold. If she were granted one wish, it would be for him to see her as more than his son's temporary part-time nanny.

Shocked at the thought, Sam pulled her hand free. "Let's buy some of this food for the animals. Tommy will love feeding them."

Tommy came rushing back when she called and Mac caught his son and lifted him high in the air before settling him against his chest. "Having fun?"

Tommy nodded and began to tell about petting the animals as if his father hadn't been watching him. He squirmed around to point out the different ones he'd patted.

Mac listened until he ran down.

"Want to feed them?" Sam asked. She held a small ice-cream cone full of the pellets. Mac put Tommy down and then stooped down beside him to hold his hand flat so the little goats could eat off his palm.

Tommy shrieked with laughter. "It tickles," he said.

Sam watched the two of them and was suddenly glad Mac had come with them. This reminded her of going with her parents and sister—a family outing. It was made more special for both her and Tommy because Mac was there.

"Ready for some hot chocolate?" He looked at Sam. "I am. Then we'll hit the highlights of the rest of the zoo and find a warm place to eat lunch. Snow is predicted for later this evening. If the temperatures stay so low, I wonder how the animals will cope."

"I'm sure the zoo has arrangements for the weather. But I bet some of them are surprised to find it colder than the African veldt," she replied.

The rest of the morning passed swiftly. Tommy laughed at the monkeys and then made faces at the wise-looking gorillas. He wanted to pet the elephant and threw a short-lived tantrum when Mac said he couldn't.

They decided to eat at one of the places opened in the

zoo, and then browse for a keepsake for Tommy—like a stuffed elephant.

The drive back was different. Tommy fell asleep almost before they left the parking lot. The silence was cozy rather than awkward. Sam felt pleasantly tired, but not at all sleepy. She had dinner to prepare when she returned home. She'd thought she would have Tommy underfoot all afternoon, but since his father was home, she wouldn't.

"You're still coming to dinner, aren't you?" she asked when Mac turned onto his street.

"Wouldn't miss it."

"I thought to make spaghetti if you like that. It's something we can cook on our camp stove, and I know Tommy likes it."

"Camp stove?"

"I told you that a large old oak fell through the back of our house during Hurricane George. It pretty much destroyed our kitchen. We've been cooking on a camp stove until we can afford repairs."

Mac frowned. He knew the hurricane had damaged her home; she'd said that was the reason for the second job. But he hadn't realized they were still impacted by it. "Hurricane George was months ago."

"I explained that before," she murmured.

"I thought you were paying off repairs, not waiting to get them."

"We had the roof repaired and that's what we're paying off. Next on our agenda is the kitchen. Maybe by spring, with the lavish salary you're paying me, we'll be able to get that repaired."

He said nothing, soon turning into the long driveway to his home.

"Come in and get warm before heading home," he suggested.

"Maybe for a minute. Need any help with Tommy?"

"I can manage. If he doesn't wake up when I take him out

of the car seat, I'll put him in bed to nap as long as he wants. Today was exciting for him and I think he might stay asleep for a long while."

He did just as Mac thought.

Sam waited in the foyer while Mac took Tommy up to bed, and then returned.

"Coffee?"

She nodded and followed him into the kitchen, where a moment later he realized there was no water coming from the faucet.

"Odd," he said, trying both the hot and cold. A trickle came from the hot, soon diminishing to a drip.

"Pipes frozen, I bet," she said. "It's cold enough."

"As long as they don't burst," he said, heading downstairs to the basement. The area was cooler than the rest of the house, but not as cold as outside. The pipes looked fine.

He joined Sam in the kitchen. "If they are frozen, it's outside somewhere."

"So I'll pass on the coffee."

"With Tommy sleeping upstairs, I can't run out to a coffee bar," he said, slowly, stepping closer, invading her space. Sam resisted her inclination to step back. Her heart pounded. She studied his dark eyes, wishing for things unknown. It had been a long time since she'd felt special feelings for a man. She had her heart set on moving west, but until then, she wouldn't mind a little companionship—more than her sister provided.

"I should be going home," she said a second later. Should, but didn't want to.

"Thanks for suggesting the zoo. Tommy had fun."

"I did, too."

"Me, too," he said, leaning over to brush his lips against hers. "We'll be at your place at six."

Sam nodded and left, proud of the way she walked and didn't run to her car.

* * *

By six o'clock Sam was a nervous wreck. The sauce was simmering on the camp stove burner. Water boiling for the spaghetti noodles. She'd told her sister she was inviting the McAlhenys and received a boatload of questions—starting with should Charlene admit she'd been the one to strongly encourage Sam to use the ticket.

"Should I thank him for giving you a job, or would that be awkward since he got you fired from the other one?" she asked.

"I'd made a big deal about getting fired, now I don't want flak about taking a job with the man. I still feel a bit funny about it. I know he offered because he felt guilty. He didn't deliberately get me fired. Just treat him like Timothy Parsons when I had him to dinner last summer."

"We had a working kitchen then," Charlene murmured, studying her sister. "As I expect Mr. McAlheny does. So why invite them here?"

"For a home-cooked meal," Sam said, ignoring the fact Mrs. Horton cooked for them every day.

"And he's coming here to dinner, with water-stained ceilings and a kitchen that's half gone? A dining room that looks like a sewing factory and dinner in the living room?" Charlene looked at Sam as if she'd lost her mind.

Sam shrugged. "Thank goodness Ruth next door let us use her oven. I'd hate to offer spaghetti without hot garlic bread."

"Hey, pancakes would have been fine," Charlene teased, mentioning a meal they'd eaten a lot of over the past few months. Apparently realizing her sister wasn't going to answer the other questions, she stopped pushing.

"Tommy would love that, I'm sure," Sam said.

"I can't wait to meet him. I hope the chair won't put him off. We've never been much around kids, even when we were little—except ourselves."

Sam shrugged. "That's what happens with small families."

"So go get married and give me lots of nieces and nephews," Charlene said.

Sam shrugged again. Did her sister have no expectations of marriage and kids herself? Would it be possible? They'd never discussed it. Sam felt a new sense of sadness at the thought of her sister never having a family of her own. Even if she couldn't give birth, adoption was an option.

Only, Charlene went out even less than Sam—and she hadn't had a date that Sam knew of since the accident almost ten years ago. Her older sister had been popular in high school and college. It wasn't fair. Some man was missing out on a wonderful, loving woman.

Maybe instead of selling her patterns and quilted goods, Sam should be brainstorming ideas for Charlene to meet eligible men.

But not tonight, she thought as the doorbell sounded.

Mac held Tommy as they entered. Sam introduced everyone. The little boy looked around at their house, his eyes opening wide when he spotted Charlene. He tilted his head slightly to take in the chair and the woman sitting in it.

"Does that move?" he asked.

"It sure does," Charlene said. "Want a ride?"

Tommy nodded and struggled to get down. Mac put him on his feet and peeled off his jacket before turning him loose.

Charlene leaned over and lifted Tommy to her lap. "Sit still and off we go," she said, turning the chair and heading for the dining room.

"Is that allowed?" Mac asked quietly when Sam reached for Tommy's jacket. She hung it up in the closet and then took Mac's.

"Why not? I think it would be very cool if I were a kid. It's only if you know she'll never get out of the chair that it becomes more sad than fun."

"It was nice of her to offer," he said. He handed her a bouquet of flowers.

"They're lovely. Thank you," she said, smelling the crisp cinnamon scent of carnations and touching the mums with gentle fingers. "I love fresh cut flowers," she said. How long had it been since anyone had given her flowers? She thought it might have been forever.

"Something smells delicious," Mac said.

"Good. I need to run next door to get the garlic bread and then we'll be ready to eat in a jiffy. What happened with your pipes?"

"I called a plumber, but he couldn't get out today. Said pipes are freezing all over the city, apparently this cold is so bad and long it's penetrating the soil."

"Yikes. We're lucky then, to still have running water."

"Sounds like you deserve a break after George. Can I see the kitchen?"

"Come on back."

When they passed through the dining room, Mac stopped to look at the projects underway: the finished quilts and clothing on one side and the large quilting frame set up for sewing. "I have a friend who would love this. Maybe she can come over sometime," he said, fingering one of the wall hangings Charlene had done. "She's into this kind of stuff."

"She'd be welcome. I love talking about quilting. Unfortunately my sister tolerates it only. She'd rather be out in the wilderness talking about mountain lions," Charlene said with a teasing look at Sam.

Mac raised an eyebrow and turned to look at Sam. "Mountain lions?"

"An old dream. Come on back." She felt a pang thinking about the wildlife talks she could have given over the years, if things had been different. But they weren't and most of the time she really didn't regret the lost opportunity. Like when she was asleep.

Mac followed her into the kitchen, leaving Tommy talking a mile a minute to Charlene as they headed back toward the living room in her wheelchair.

"Whoa, this is a mess. How have you two managed all these months?" he said when he saw the plywood-covered opening, the gaping space where a range had once stood.

The back of the room was boarded up with plywood. The destroyed stove and other debris had been removed. The room was drafty and cold. The tree had missed the sink, but it was still old with chipped enamel. Nothing like the modern open floor kitchen he had.

The camp stove she'd talked about sat on a makeshift table near the wall, a pot of spaghetti sauce bubbling merrily in one pot. Water boiling for the noodles threw steam up from the second pot.

"It wasn't very bad before it got so cold. The roof was of more importance. I told you about messing up with the insurance coverage. I rectified it immediately, but it wasn't retroactive. We almost have that roof repair paid off. Then we can see about getting in a contractor for bids on this work and start saving for that."

"I know a couple of guys who might give you a good deal," he said, walking around the perimeter assessing the damage.

"I'll be glad to have them. I know nothing about this kind of thing. We think now we'll wait until spring. It's cold enough in here with the plywood—can you imagine how cold it would be with no wall for a few days?"

"You two could stay at my place," he said.

She spun around and looked at him in surprise. "You don't know us well enough to make such an offer."

He looked back. "I just did. What does length of acquaintance have to do with it? I have known some people for decades who I would not want in my house."

"Thanks for the offer, but Charlene has special needs. This place is set up for her. We'll be fine." Sam turned back to add the spaghetti noodles to the boiling water. For a few seconds she could imagine staying at Mac's lavish home. She'd seen the bathrooms, Huge in comparison to their own. She had explored the house one evening after Tommy went to sleep, and could picture herself staying in the guest bedroom with the lovely old-fashioned bed and en suite bath.

But his house wasn't set up for a handicapped person so they would not be staying with Mac.

"I'll have the names and phone numbers for you on Monday," he said.

"Okay, thanks. Can you watch this? Just give it a stir in a minute, I'll be right back."

Sam dashed to the neighbors to get the bread as soon as she put the noodles in the boiling water. By the time she returned, dinner was ready.

She and Charlene had set up a table in the living room to eat—where it was warmer than at the table in the kitchen. The fire in the fireplace gave it a nice ambiance and Sam turned down the lighting so the well-worn look wasn't as evident.

Tommy loved the spaghetti. To Sam's delight, so did his father.

The evening went better than expected, with Charlene coming out of her shell and talking easily with Mac and Tommy. Mac didn't seem the least bit off put by Charlene's situation, which pleased Sam no end.

There was only ice cream for dessert, but Tommy relished every spoonful.

"Thank you for dinner," Mac said when they finished. "I had better get Tommy home before he falls asleep in the empty ice-cream bowl."

Charlene glanced at Sam. "Why don't you walk them out? I'll clear the table."

"We can help," Mac offered.

"No, thanks. I have my own method," she said easily.

Sam was surprised at how her sister had blossomed during the McAlhenys' visit. She wasn't falling for Mac, was she? For a moment Sam felt almost sick. What if her sister fell in love with him? He had been kind to her over dinner, but she didn't see any special interest in his eyes. Not like when he looked at her.

The thought caught her by surprise. She had no illusions about an affair with her boss. But the odd feelings she had if she imagined her sister with him caused her concern. She would do nothing to stand in Charlene's way of happiness.

"See us to the door, but not outside. It's even colder now than during the daylight," Mac said as he bundled Tommy up in his jacket and mittens. He donned his own jacket and glanced back at the dining room. Charlene was no longer there. He turned and looked at Sam.

"Thanks for having us to dinner," he said, leaning over and brushing his lips against hers.

Sam wanted the kiss to last longer. She was growing to expect them. Maybe they should part more often; it seemed to engender kisses now. She leaned down to hug Tommy. "Stay warm," she said, afraid to look at Mac lest he see something she didn't want to reveal in her expression.

In moments they were gone. The cold had blown in with the opened door and she was glad she wasn't going out in it tonight.

When she carried some of the remaining dishes from dinner into the kitchen, Charlene was humming as she wrapped the leftover food before placing in the refrigerator. She looked up at Sam.

"Wow, he's something else!"

"Who, Tommy?" Sam asked, avoiding her sister's searching gaze.

"No, silly, Mac. He's the one who danced divinely at the ball, right?"

Sam nodded, not wanting to get into what else he did divinely.

"That Tommy is as cute as can be. How old did you say he was?" Charlene asked.

"Three. I'm not sure when his next birthday is." Sam thought she should find out. If he celebrated his fourth birthday while she was still working for his father, she'd want to do something for him.

"If I were a walking woman, I'd go for him myself," Charlene said.

Sam turned and glared at her sister. "There's no reason for you not to become involved with anyone you want. Walking is not the only thing that defines a person."

"I know, I'm just saying most men don't want to be tied down with a cripple."

"There's more to you than that. You're funny, intelligent, talented, creative—"

"Whoa, sis. Thanks for the great endorsement, but let's face it. I'm never going to get married."

Sam felt her eyes fill with tears at Charlene's statement.

"That's not true, but you would have to go out a bit more," she said, blinking and turning away.

"So it's up to you to get married and give me lots of kids to play with."

Sam brushed her cheeks and began to run the hot water to wash the dishes.

"I'm not getting married—at least not for years. If I can swing it, I still want to work out west. Once the repairs are made, it'll only take another year to get my degree. Then, watch out."

Charlene put the rest of the food into the refrigerator and moved over to be near Sam.

"I'm holding you back. If it weren't for me, you would have fulfilled your dream years ago."

"You don't know that. Besides, everything happens for a reason. This way, I'll be more mature, more certain what I want, and have lots more experience dealing with people than I would have at twenty-one."

"Don't you want to get married?" Charlene asked.

"One day, maybe. I might meet a fellow ranger and we can be married at one of the parks."

"Oh. I thought you could fall for Mac and have an instant family for me to spoil."

"Too much baggage. I couldn't do all I need to do if a young child was involved. I'd have to spend time with him for years and that would set me back even more."

"Don't you like Tommy?"

"Of course, who wouldn't?" Sam felt like a Scrooge calling Tommy baggage. But she knew what would happen if she fell for a man who had a family to care for. She'd be tied down even longer. She wouldn't be able to walk away to pursue her dream.

Keep that thought firmly in mind, she told herself. No more wishing for kisses from Mac McAlheny. She needed to focus on her goal and not get sidetracked by a sexy guy who could kiss like no one else she'd ever known and who sent her heart into spins every time she thought about him.

"I know you've had your goal of a job out west since you were a teenager. If it hadn't been for the crash, you would have had years of service under your belt by now. But don't close your mind to other forms of happiness because you are too focused on your goal. National park rangers have families and friends. They own homes and take vacations and live normal lives."

"I know that. But they don't have a spouse two thousand miles away, which is how it would end up if I got involved with someone from Atlanta."

Charlene didn't say any more and in a few moments moved back to the dining room.

Sam finished the dishes trying to keep her mind a blank. She did not want to dwell on might-have-beens. Or could be. Life was as it was. She never would have met Mac if she hadn't used that ticket. Closing her eyes, she could see the expansive vistas of the western parks—soaring mountains snowcapped all year long, or distant horizons with a hundred-mile view. That's where she wanted to be. Learning all she could about the history and natural resources that made the places so special. Walking the land where Indians had once roamed and the cavalry had ridden.

She was not going to get sidetracked by falling for some man who had a darling little boy. A child who would not understand why a mommy lived so far away.

Not that Mac had given any indication of moving beyond the boss/nanny scenario they now had. Except, maybe, for the kisses.

CHAPTER SIX

SUNDAY evening Sam was about to take a quick shower before bed when the phone rang.

"Sam? It's Mac. The water pipes are worse than first thought. They burst near the water main at the street this morning. We have a real mess out front, as do several of the neighbors. And no water. An estimated three days before everything is restored. You and Mrs. Horton can't work here with no water, so I'm taking some time off from work and will get a hotel room for Tommy and me."

"Don't do that," she said. "You offered me a place to stay, let me return the offer. We have four bedrooms upstairs that aren't being used at all. I can't volunteer Charlene to watch Tommy, but I bet she won't mind if Mrs. Horton watches him here during the day and I'll be home evenings to take over."

"I can't impose like that."

"It's no imposition. I know Charlene would love the company. She was captivated by Tommy last night. And so far our water is flowing."

"Be careful what you say, you'll jinx it."

She laughed, suddenly feeling inexplicably happy. "Come on over. You can even have the first shower in the morning."

There was a pause, then Mac said, "Thank you, Sam. We will take you up on the offer."

* * *

Mac replaced the phone and remained at the study desk. He had other resources. He could even take Tommy to stay with Chris's parents or his own for a few days. They'd love to have their grandson visit. But both sets of grandparents lived in Savannah and he didn't want Tommy to be so far away.

He could have taken a few days off and found a motel for them both. Staying with strangers hadn't figured in his plans. Yet when she'd offered, he hadn't thought about it for long before accepting.

Now what? Was he getting into a relationship that would prove sticky to get out of?

Leaning back, he considered the ramifications. Which he should have done before. He was content with his life, with the casual dates and superficial relationships he'd had over the past couple of years.

Was that changing?

What message was he giving by staying with Sam and her sister? Especially when he had friends of long standing who would put him and Tommy up in a heartbeat. Why hadn't he called them?

It wasn't too late. But even as he had the thought, he reached for the phone to call Mrs. Horton and let her know about the change of venue for the next couple of days. He just hoped Tommy wouldn't be too much trouble and wear out their welcome before the pipes were repaired.

Monday morning Sam waited for Mac and Tommy to arrive before leaving for work. It continued to be cold and now snow was predicted. She'd talked to Charlene about Tommy's being watched at their home for a few days. She said little about his daytime caregiver and hoped her sister could get along with Mrs. Horton.

Of course, the nanny arrived first. She glanced around the

entryway and frowned at Sam. "Does Mr. McAlheny expect me to clean this place while I'm here?"

"Not at all," Sam said defensively. Maybe the home did not meet Mrs. Horton's impossible standards, but it was clean and tidy and more suitable, in Sam's opinion, to a young boy's exuberant activities than his own home.

Her sister glided into the foyer to meet Mrs. Horton. For a moment Sam worried the older woman would make some unkind remark, but she merely shook hands and began to take off her coat. Her eyes caught a glimpse into the dining room at the array of fabric spilled over the table and she stopped and stepped closer for a better look.

"Quilting?" she asked, her gaze roaming over the various projects hanging from the wall, or spread on adjacent tables.

"I quilt," Charlene said.

"As do I. Only not as good as this!" Mrs. Horton, still wearing her coat, walked into the room and began exclaiming over some of the art pieces Charlene had created. She stopped before one of a garden as if seen through a leaded glass window.

"This is breathtaking," she said, tilting her head and studying every stitch. "I wish I could do something this lovely. What a talent you have. I envy you."

Sam looked at her sister in surprise. Who would have thought dour Mrs. Horton could have such passion?

"I have a pattern," Charlene offered, wheeling over next to Mrs. Horton. "And I'd be glad to help you get started."

"I should love that," Mrs. Horton said, giving the first smile Sam had ever seen.

Sam heard voices outside and went to the door to open it before Mac could ring the bell.

"Mrs. Horton is already here," she said as she welcomed them into the foyer.

"She's always punctual," Mac said.

"Where's Charlene?" Tommy asked. "I want another ride."

Samantha laughed at his excitement and reached down to unfasten his coat and help him out of it. "She's in the quilting room with Mrs. Horton. Wait until they finish talking, okay?"

"Okay." He ran into the room and Sam rose, putting Tommy's jacket over the knob to the closet. She looked at Mac.

"How's the water situation?"

"Major repairs are now underway on the street. The agency was on the job before we left, digging up the asphalt, a dozen men standing around waiting to work when they can get to the pipes. In the meantime, there's slush bubbling up from the break."

"It's still freezing out and expected to grow colder," she said. "And I hear snow is coming. Did you bring suitcases?"

"They're in the car. I'll bring them in now."

Sam closed the door against the cold when Mac left, watching through the small glass panes near the top of the door. When he returned, two suitcases were all he brought.

"Where to?" he asked.

Sam led the way upstairs, already nervous about the sleeping arrangements. She'd cleaned her parents' room thoroughly after Mac's call and made up the bed with fresh linens. That would do for Mac. The room next to hers she'd prepared for Tommy. She showed him the rooms. His was opposite hers. With the doors open, they could look directly into each room.

"Nice."

"Ignore the water stain on the ceiling. Another gift from George," she said, looking at the room with nostalgia. Sam had rearranged the furniture, bought a new bed and repainted after her parents' death. They'd hoped their aunt Lila would come live with them, but she retired to Florida and had died less than two years after her sister. The room had never been used since Sam's remodeling.

Mac put one suitcase by the bed and studied the ceiling for a moment.

"You know, Samantha, I might be able to help you a bit, in exchange for letting us stay here. I know a bit about repair work."

"Like?"

"Like it looks as if it would only take a couple of sheets of drywall, and some new paint, to repair this problem. Unless something is damaged above in the attic."

"No. We had the house inspected after the hurricane, and got a list of all problems. The rafters are sound, the water didn't sit—it poured through."

"The main damage was to the kitchen," he said, turning and carrying Tommy's suitcase.

She showed him the smaller room next to hers and they headed back downstairs. She entered the living room beneath the master bedroom and gestured to the ceiling in the corner.

"That's stained as well. It's not as noticeable because it didn't get as wet."

"Easy fixes. What else?"

"Can you do kitchens?" she asked wistfully.

He shrugged. "We can look at it and decide the best strategy."

Her hopes soared. Then plunged. She didn't even have enough money saved to buy the supplies and she did not want to get into debt. "We'll discuss it later. I have to get to work now."

Checking on Tommy proved he was well taken care of by Mrs. Horton and Charlene. Sam was surprised by how different Mrs. Horton looked when she spoke with her sister and Tommy. Maybe she just didn't like her!

"Can I drop you at work?" Mac asked as they walked outside a few moments later. "The roads are slippery."

"Thanks, but I need the car later."

"I'll come straight back after work, to make sure Tommy doesn't make a nuisance of himself," Mac said.

"Okay, I'll see you for dinner, then." She left with a glow she hadn't felt in a long time. How foolish, just because she knew ahead of time she'd be eating with Mac and Tommy.

Sam could hardly concentrate on work. Twice in the morning she called home to see how things were going.

Both times her sister told her everything was fine. "Instead of only Alice watching him, he has two women. But I'm going to have to get new rubber for the wheels if we keep riding around like this."

Sam could tell from the tone of voice that Charlene was having a great time.

"Who's Alice?" she asked.

"Alice Horton, the woman who watches Tommy during the day." Charlene sounded as if she thought Sam had lost her marbles.

"Oh, I didn't know her first name."

"Mmm, did you ever ask?" Charlene said.

Sam didn't reply to that. "Well, I just wanted to make sure Tommy wasn't too much."

Hanging up, she debated calling Mac, but it was a trumped-up excuse at best, so she didn't. For some reason, thinking of them staying with her for a few days changed things. She felt more proprietary about Mac and Tommy.

She tried to focus on the project at hand, but thoughts of Mac kept interfering. She remembered how terrific he looked at the zoo. He was definitely high on the masculine chart, yet was gentle with his son. He wasn't afraid to show his love for Tommy.

What would it be like to have him turn those brown eyes on her with the same expression? She shivered slightly at the thought. She already knew what kissing him was like.

How would living with him be? Not that she was exactly *living* with him—he was just staying with her and her sister until his water pipes were repaired. But surely there'd be a few moments when Mac and she would be alone. Would she learn more about the man, or end up stealing kisses?

Sam rose, determined to get those fantasies out of her mind. She had work to do—here and at home. She was still Tommy's nanny in the evenings. Mac might come home tonight to make sure Tommy was all right at her place, but that wasn't going to be the norm.

Despite telling herself a dozen times during the day to forget about Mac, she left work promptly at five in a state of high anticipation. She could not wait to see him again!

Arriving home later than expected due to traffic delays because of weather, Sam was surprised to see Mrs. Horton still sitting on the sofa with Tommy, talking with Charlene. She looked up in surprise. "Is it time to go already?" she asked.

Sam blinked. Usually the woman met her at the door in her coat.

"It's a bit after six. I'm sorry to be late…the roads are treacherous," she said, taking off her coat and reaching down to give Tommy a hug when he struggled down from the sofa and ran over to her. He began telling her something about a truck but once again his enthusiasm ran away with his words and Sam was hard-pressed to understand much.

"I'll run up and change and then get dinner started," Sam said. She hoped she didn't show the disappointment that Mac hadn't returned yet. Maybe he had decided to work late after all. A dozen things could have come up to delay him.

"I need to be going," Alice Horton said. "I'll just make it to class as it is. But the time flew by."

"I look forward to tomorrow," Charlene replied. "Tommy and I will see you out."

Sam bid the woman goodbye and then ran lightly up the steps. She swiftly changed into warm pants and a thick sweater. Even with the heat from the camp stove, the kitchen was cold. She had just turned the knob on her door when Tommy knocked.

Opening it, she smiled down at him.

"Charlene said find me a sweater, I'm cold."

"Of course I will, sweetie, come on." They went into the guest room where Tommy was staying and Sam found a warm sweater for the little boy.

"Pictures," he said as they began walking toward the stairs. He darted into her room and gazed at the large posters she had all around. Arches National Park and Rocky Mountain, Glacier, Yosemite. All the ones she someday hoped to work in. She loved the vistas the posters displayed. It had been years since she put them up, but she never got tired of the views.

"Tommy?"

Mac stood in the doorway. He smiled as his son raced across the room and flung himself into his daddy's arms. Standing, Mac looked at Sam. "I hope he wasn't making a pest of himself."

"Not at all. He was just looking at the pictures." She gestured a bit self-consciously. How many grown women had posters all over their walls?

"They're pretty," he said, stepping in another couple of feet so he could see them all. Mac took his time studying each one. Then he turned his eyes to the bed Sam slept in. It was not the frilly feminine kind he might have pictured. The dark blue quilt hung to the floor. There were several pillows to snuggle against if she wanted to read in bed. The lighting was prefect for that.

He glanced at her and saw her still gazing at the posters.

"All national parks out west," he guessed. Most had names blazoned across the bottom.

She nodded. "One day I want to be a park ranger."

"One day?"

"That's what I'm working on my degree for. If I can get a good job, I can afford to take Charlene with me."

"You want to leave Atlanta?" he asked. The thought surprised him. It showed how little he knew about her.

Sam nodded. "I would have left years ago if not for my sister—not that it's her fault of course, but she needed me around. So instead of graduating from college when I might have done, I'm still slogging away. But one day…" She trailed off as she smiled at the pictures. They gave her heart a lift. She couldn't wait to see the actual scenery herself.

"I know you've mentioned this in passing," he said slowly. "But I didn't realize how solid a goal it was for you."

She looked at him. Was there something more in his tone? Did it matter to him if she left? For a moment she almost smiled. Maybe he'd miss her.

Suddenly Sam realized she'd miss him. She hardly knew him, but she already felt he was a part of her life. What would it be like when the pipes were repaired and he left? Once she had enough money for all the repairs and she would no longer need a second job?

She didn't want to think that far ahead. That would mean not seeing Mac and just the thought of that was disturbing. She stared at him, wondering if going west was the big deal she'd always made it. She was aware of every inch of the man, from his solidly planted feet to the top of his head, which just cleared under her door frame. He looked breathtaking in his dark suit and white shirt that looked as fresh holding Tommy right now as it had that morning.

For a moment the intimacy of being in her bedroom hit her. It was as if he belonged here. Which was an odd thought. No man had ever been in her room before.

They had never done more than exchange a few kisses. But for a moment she felt as if he'd come in here a thousand times.

"I need to get supper started," she said. Mac and Tommy blocked the door. The room seemed to grow smaller. Would he come help? Instantly the image of Mac and her working together sprang to the forefront.

"I came up to find Tommy." He eyed her clothing and added, "And change before supper."

"Plenty of time. See you downstairs."

It took Sam a few moments to get her equilibrium under control when she reached the kitchen. She had no reason to want him to help her. The space was limited and she'd manage better alone—especially if she felt that anticipation and awareness every moment he was around. How could she concentrate on ingredients if she was distracted?

But what a distraction.

She laughed softly at her silliness and set to getting things ready for a meal.

When she was almost finished, she went to the archway to the dining room. The place was empty but she heard voices from the living room. They'd placed the table there to eat the other evening and would be using it until the McAlhenys left. She and Charlene usually just ate in the kitchen. It was easier for her sister.

Walking through to the living room, Sam saw Mac sitting on the floor with Tommy playing cars. Charlene was nearby, watching them as she and Mac talked.

Sam was torn. Despite herself, a small spark of jealousy rose. Yet she was delighted her sister forgot her situation long enough to talk comfortably with such a sexy guy. Maybe—

Tommy spied her and jumped up, running to her. He never seemed to walk when he could run.

"Is dinner ready?" he asked, jumping up and down.

"Yes, we just need to set the table," she replied, glancing once more at Mac.

"I can help," Tommy said.

Mac rose effortlessly, all flowing male muscles and sexy good looks. His hair was a bit mussed. The look in his eyes make her heart race. She wished she could drag him away somewhere and kiss until neither one of them knew their names. But a quick glance at Charlene convinced her she better watch her step. Her sister was studying her with a speculative expression. No sense giving credence to that growing speculation.

"Okay, come on then," Sam said to Tommy.

He beamed a smile and nodded, already heading for the kitchen.

It took a bit longer than it otherwise would have with Tommy helping, but soon they were sitting down to pork chops and rice with two vegetables. Tommy protested, but his dad told him he liked them, so the little boy was soon eating.

Sam took a bite and caught Mac's eye. The food turned to sawdust in her mouth and she couldn't look away. The slow heat that built surprised her. For heaven's sake, she was at dinner with her sister and his son. But it felt as if it were just the two of them in the world.

Making an effort to break his gaze, she quickly finished the mouthful and took a long drink of water. If that happened again, she'd never get her dinner eaten. She deliberately kept her eyes off the man until she'd had enough food. If she went gaga every time she looked at him, the entire world would soon notice—especially Mac.

That sobering thought had her reviewing all the times they'd spent together. She hadn't acted like a total idiot, had she?

Mac watched Sam as they ate. She met his gaze only once the entire meal. Was she regretting inviting him and Tommy to stay with them? Maybe he should find other accommodations for the next few days. He didn't want her to feel awkward in her own house.

Or was it that? Did he imagine the faint pink tinge to her cheeks? Maybe there was a reciprocal feeling on her side. He'd watched the clock all day in anticipation of returning to the Duncans' home. Only to be met by Sam with the information she wanted to move away from Atlanta. That was his home. The place his business was thriving. The place where he'd buried his wife. It had a special hold on his life. Now Samantha was talking about leaving.

Chris. What would she think of all this?

For a moment the ache of loss hit him again. But oddly, it didn't feel as devastating as before. More like an old injury flaring up, but not the immediate intensity of the injury. Was he finally getting over her?

Panic touched. He'd loved Chris for years and he didn't want to get over her. He wanted to mourn her all his life. They should have had fifty or sixty years together.

Instead he was staying with a newly met woman, and feeling some of the same tug of awareness he'd once felt for his wife.

Mac frowned. Staying here had been a mistake. Yet one look at Tommy's face, with his sunny smile, bright eyes and way he hung on everything Sam or Charlene said made the stay worthwhile. Mac would do anything for his son. Chris had missed so much. He ached to think she'd never seen Tommy smile, heard his laughter. Helped him get dressed, or eat. She'd missed it all.

And Tommy had missed having a mother. Louise had been wonderful, but she'd left. Mrs. Horton was temporary, even Sam was temporary. He should provide better for his son.

But to get married just to give Tommy a mother? He couldn't do that. Not after knowing and loving Chris. He needed time to think. Or to find the perfect housekeeper who would stay until Tommy grew up.

He'd interviewed one woman last week, but found fault with her. Was he being too particular? No, he rejected that thought immediately. Not where his son was concerned.

Charlene said something and Mac looked at her. "I'm sorry, I was woolgathering, I guess. What was that?"

"I was just saying how much I enjoy Alice. She's an avid quilter, you know."

Quilter? "No, I didn't know." Truth be told, he knew little beyond her references and application. He was always in a rush to leave when she arrived, and now Sam was home when he got back each night.

"We had a lovely time today when Tommy was napping." Charlene turned to Sam. "She's going to try my garden window pattern."

The talk about quilts reminded him about Chris's friend who so loved quilts. He'd have to give her a call after dinner and see if she'd come look at Charlene's work. If it was as good as it seemed to him, maybe Monica could find an outlet for some pieces which would bring in some much-needed money to this family.

Which reminded him of another project.

"I asked one of the contractors I know to check out your kitchen this week and give me some directions for things I can do. I thought I'd get started on Saturday. But I need help."

How blatant was that? If Sam had any doubts he wanted to spend the day with her, that should settle them. Though he wasn't sure she'd find working on their kitchen fun. But it would at least give them a chance to talk while they worked.

She looked at him then and smiled. "You were serious about helping," she exclaimed.

He nodded. He always kept his word.

"Thank you."

She quickly explained to her sister who joined in offering to watch Tommy so he wouldn't get in the way while they worked.

Mac thanked her, wondering how a wheelchair-bound woman would watch a rambunctious little boy like Tommy. But at least he'd just be in the kitchen, not far away if she needed him.

When dinner ended, Charlene insisted on doing the dishes. When Sam agreed, but said she'd clear the table, Mac felt free to spend time with Tommy until bed. Then he'd call Monica.

* * *

Once he put his son to bed, he went to the small room Sam had pointed out as their home office. He pulled the door shut and looked up Monica's number.

"Mac, I haven't heard from you in ages. What's going on with you? How's Tommy?" she asked after greetings had been exchanged.

"Growing as fast as he can. I'm calling for a favor. I've recently met a woman who does quilts."

"Ah, is she important?"

"Not in that way. But I think the things she's done look great and wanted an expert opinion. Would you mind?"

"Things are a bit slow now with the Christmas rush over. I could squeeze in something for an old friend. As long as I get to see you and Tommy."

"Tommy for sure. I'll try to make it."

They chatted for a little longer and Mac gave her the address. He had barely hung up when Sam knocked on the door.

He crossed over and opened it. "I was on the phone. Come in, I want to talk to you."

He took her hand, and immediately felt a tingling awareness that caught him unaware. Shutting the door, he leaned against it and pulled her into his arms. "I really did want to discuss something with you, but it'll have to wait." Lowering his head, he kissed her.

For a moment he thought she wouldn't respond, but in only seconds, Sam pushed against him, encircling his neck with her arms and kissing him back for all she was worth. It was spectacular. Endless time floated by as he felt her body stretched against his, the sweetness of her mouth. Her tongue danced with his as they extended the kiss.

Finally they were both breathing hard. He rested his forehead on hers, gazing down into her warm brown eyes.

She smiled at him, dreamily. He felt desire sweep through him like lightning. He wanted her. He hadn't felt anything like this in years, maybe ever. It was as if his next breath depended on Sam being in his life.

"That's some discussion," she murmured.

"Oh, yeah, that." Slowly he released her, making sure she was steady before pushing away from the door and stepping away. He needed some space if he was going to be able to think.

He told her about Monica and her agreement to visit and see if Charlene's quilts were something she could sell.

"What do you mean?" Sam asked, suddenly wary.

"Monica has a fashionable boutique in the Galleria. She agreed to see if she could do anything with Charlene's work."

"You asked her without checking with us first?"

"If Monica says no, there's no harm done," he said easily. Why was Sam getting upset?

"Do you know how long it's been since Charlene was in that accident? Almost ten years. In all that time she has never tried to sell a quilt. I think her work is beautiful, exquisite. But what if not everyone agrees with me? Think how her self-esteem will be shattered if your friend waltzes in and declares them not worthy."

He leveled a gaze at her. "What if she comes in and thinks the pieces are as exquisite as you and I do? What if she can sell them and provide a source of income for Charlene?"

Sam stared at him, slowly allowing the idea to enter her mind. He could almost see the wheels turning.

"Talk about a booster," he continued. "If she sells one or two quilts, or those arty pieces she does so well, don't you think that'll go a long way to her own acceptance of being in the wheelchair? You can't think she can't do it, not with where you work and how you enable disabled people to find all kinds of jobs."

"Of course she can do it," Sam said fiercely. "I'm afraid of her being hurt."

"Being hurt is part of life. It's what we do when setbacks

happen that makes us grow. I don't think Monica would say one word to hurt your sister. I think she'd be as delighted with the pieces as you and I are."

"Why would you do this?" Sam asked, still studying him as if he were some new, exotic species.

"You're helping us out by putting us up while our pipes are repaired. It's not that big a deal."

"Oh, yes, it is," she said, coming over and reaching up to pull his head down for another kiss. Her palms on his cheeks were warm. Her lips moist and hot. He was drowning in sensation from her kiss. What would it be like to make love to Sam? To sweep her into his arms and carry her upstairs and close a bedroom door behind them?

Mac groaned with the image and pulled back. There was only so much a man could stand. There'd be no taking her into some bedroom while Tommy was sleeping nearby, or her sister was in the house. What was he thinking?

"Are you okay?" she asked when he broke their embrace.

Mac paced to the opposite end of the small room and nodded. It was obvious—he hadn't been thinking—only feeling. And wishing.

"When is Monica coming?" she asked, sitting on the edge of the large old desk.

"She's going to try tomorrow or the next day. I figured she'll pop in, check out the merchandise and then take any she can sell—even if she only takes one to make sure Charlene's feelings aren't hurt. She was a friend of my wife's. She's not going to hurt your sister, I'm sure of it. I'm hoping she can help."

Sam swung her legs slightly, banging them softly into the side of the desk. "So do we tell Charlene beforehand or not?"

"Your call—you know her better. I'd say I have a friend stopping by to see her quilts. Let it go from there."

"Okay. She and Alice Horton sure enjoyed talking quilts today. I've never seen your housekeeper so animated."

He tilted his head slightly, a puzzled frown marring his features. "Alice Horton animated? I thought that was mutually exclusive."

Sam giggled and then frowned at him. "Don't be mean. She's not warm and friendly, but I think she's a really nice woman."

"She has excellent references."

"Is that how you judge everyone, by their references?" she asked.

"No." He stepped closer. "You didn't have any, as I recall."

Her eyes danced in amusement as he drew near. Like a moth to flame—he couldn't resist. She was flirting with him, and he loved it.

"Shall I provide you with some now?" she asked, the look in her eyes making his heart skip a beat.

"Too late, I already spoke with your boss, Timothy Parsons. He raves about you."

Another step and he could reach out and touch her. But he held back, extending the anticipation. She looked him up and down. She was deliberately provoking him.

"It's too bad bosses don't come with references, then I could read up on you," she said.

When he reached for her she spun away, almost falling off the desk, laughter ringing out. "Maybe I don't have references on you, but I could see that coming a mile away," she teased, dancing out of reach.

With a mock growl, he cornered her and put a hand on the wall on either side of her head. "Now what?" he asked.

"Your call," she said, touching his chest, rubbing her fingers over the sweater he wore. When she looked up at him, he was lost.

The kiss went on forever—or was that merely wishful thinking on his part?

CHAPTER SEVEN

OKAY, she was in dangerous territory, Sam thought a moment later. The kiss had been wild and wanton, stopping just short of indecent when she pushed gently against him.

"I have a sister who could come in at any minute," she said. Sorry to put the brakes on things, Sam was nothing if not conscientious.

This man was her boss—kind of. At least while she was hired to watch his son.

"I think I'll go tell Charlene your friend Monica will be coming by." Sam couldn't meet Mac's eyes. She felt flustered and uncertain.

She couldn't have a crush on her new boss! The job was only temporary—until she had enough money to finish the repairs on the house. And nothing good ever came from wishing for the unattainable.

He let her escape without any protest and Sam ducked into the downstairs bathroom to splash cool water on her face and try to erase that just-kissed look. Her sister would spot it in a heartbeat. It would take a while for her eyes to lose the dazed expression, she thought. She wanted to hug herself with the delight but didn't want to intrigue Charlene too much.

Sam finally went to find Charlene and let her know about the expected visitor, then fled to bed. Sleep was hard to come, however. Reliving the kiss kept her in a high state of longing for more. Mac was the most dynamic man she knew and falling for him would be pure folly. He was still hung up on his wife. Hadn't he said Monica was a friend of his wife's? He obviously still thought of Chris as in the present.

Besides, she thought as she turned on her side, just able to see the rim of the Grand Canyon poster with the street-lights, she had her own future and it did not include becoming involved with a man and his child and staying in Atlanta. She had wide-open spaces to visit, ecosystems to learn about.

But when she fell asleep, it was with the thought of Mac McAlheny and his kisses.

Mac had already left the house the next morning before Sam went downstairs. She wasn't late, despite the lateness of the hour when she fell asleep. Taking a deep drink of hot coffee, she willed the caffeine to take effect and make her alert. She wondered if he felt awkward this morning and that's why he'd left early. She wasn't sure how she would have met him, so was glad for the reprieve.

"Want breakfast?" Charlene asked as she glided into the kitchen.

"No time. We're having a staff meeting at ten and I have a bunch of charts to finish up," Sam said. She welcomed the distraction at work. Maybe she could get through the day without thinking of Mac.

No such luck. He called at nine.

"Would you have dinner with me on Friday?" he asked.

"Dinner?" she repeated.

"Did I get you at a bad time?"

"No. Wouldn't we eat dinner at my house?"

"If the water pipes aren't repaired by then the City of Atlanta needs a new work crew. We'll be at our place and I thought a thank-you dinner would be in order."

"For me and Charlene?" Of course he would include her sister. They were both his hostesses at the house.

"If she'd like to come."

"She probably won't," Sam said. "She doesn't like going around in public if she can avoid it."

"Then just you and me."

"You don't need to do this," she said slowly, already anticipating a quiet dinner for two at some elegant restaurant where perhaps there'd be dancing?

"It's the least I can do to thank you for your hospitality. I was going to ask last night, but got—sidetracked."

She smiled, thinking about how they'd gotten sidetracked. "Very well, then, I accept."

"We can work out details tonight when I get home," he said.

"Okay." When she replaced the receiver, she wondered why he had to call this morning. He could have waited until this evening to ask her. Unless he didn't want to wait that long to hear her voice—like she was glad she hadn't had to wait that long to hear his.

The charts awaited, but Sam wished she didn't have to work this morning. She wished instead that she could have had a leisurely breakfast with Mac, with Tommy being miraculously watched by her sister and Alice and no one to interrupt.

When the fantasy grew out of control, she glanced around to make sure no one was around and then plunged back into the work that needed to be completed prior to the meeting. She could end up wasting the entire day thinking about her temporary houseguest.

There was a strange car in the driveway when Sam returned home that evening. She recognized Alice Horton's vehicle. Mac wasn't back yet. Who was visiting? One of Charlene's quilting guild members?

Entering the home a moment later, Sam heard voices in the dining room. She hung up her coat and then walked to the dining room, amazed at the sight in front of her. It looked as if Charlene had every item she'd ever made spread out on every available surface. Patterns were pinned to each one, except the two that were spread out over the old dining table. Alice and a woman Sam didn't know were studying the designs as Charlene explained them. Tommy was sitting beneath the table, quietly playing with some small trucks.

"Hello?" Sam said.

Tommy scrambled from under the table and ran to her. She picked him up and hugged him, smiling at the others.

"Oh my gosh, is it that late?" Charlene asked.

"Where did the time go?" Alice said, standing up and looking around as if just remembering where she was.

The sleek, sophisticated woman leaning on the table looked up and smiled at Sam.

"You must be Samantha," she said. "I'm Monica Shaw, Mac's friend. I owe him big-time. These are fantastic."

Sam glanced around. "The quilts."

"Of course the quilts. And the clothing and the artwork and best of all are the patterns. Your sister is sitting on a gold mine, and I plan to tap it for all it's worth."

Charlene's smile was the biggest Sam had ever seen. "She thinks they'll sell," she said shyly.

Alice laughed. "That's an understatement. Monica thinks they'll sell for big bucks and wants all Charlene can do—an exclusive. The details still have to be worked out."

"Fantastic!" Sam was thrilled by the news, and suddenly grateful for Mac's call to his friend. She knew her sister's work was good and now the entire city of Atlanta would know it, too.

Monica checked her watch. "I guess I need to get going. My store manager will think I died or something. But I'll be back in the morning, around nine?"

"Fine," Charlene said with a bemused air. "I'll be here."

"I need to get going, too," Alice said.

"Stay for dinner. There's so much to talk about," Charlene said.

"Oh. Well, I guess I could." Alice looked uncertain.

"There's nothing waiting for you at home. You said they cancelled the class due to the weather. Please stay."

Sam walked Monica to the door, thanking her for coming by.

"I should thank you and Mac. The work is amazing. I'm so excited. To have an exclusive line everyone will lust after is what shopkeepers dream about. Your sister is very talented."

She gave a wave and headed out, just as Mac turned into the driveway. Sam closed the door against the cold, wishing she could have kept it open to see how they greeted each other. Just as casual friends—or something more? After all, Monica had known Chris.

"Forget it, Sam, he's out of your league," she murmured.

Tommy jabbered something. Sam nuzzled him as she walked back to the dining room where Alice and Charlene were. "I want to hear all about it, but Mac just came home. Maybe you should just tell us both at once, so you don't have to repeat yourself," she said.

"I wouldn't mind repeating myself a dozen times, but I'll wait until dinner," Charlene said. "I'm thrilled with everything right now."

"I'll change quickly and fix something fast," Sam said.

Sam carried Tommy upstairs. "Come with me while I change and you can help me fix dinner."

The suggestion met with Tommy's complete approval.

Sam changed into warm slacks and another sweater and took Tommy's hand as they began to descend the stairs. He jumped from step to step. He loved the game.

Mac entered and looked up the stairs at them. He'd been talking that long with Monica? Not that Sam was timing him.

"You two look happy," he said as he watched Tommy jump again, demanding that Mac watch him.

"I am watching," his dad said as he took off his coat and tossed it over the railing.

When Tommy was a couple of steps from the bottom he

launched himself forward, pulling out of Sam's grip. Mac caught him and spun him around.

"Good grief, I thought he was going to fall," she said, leaning against the banister and watching them.

"He thinks he can fly. I hope I'm always there to catch him," Mac said, placing Tommy on the floor and watching as he ran into the dining room.

"I spoke with Monica," he said as Sam descended the last few steps. "It's good news, isn't it?"

"Thank you so much for calling her. It seems unreal she likes Charlene's quilts so much. My sister said she'd give us the entire story at dinner. Which I'm off to make right now."

"Need some help?" He looked at her mouth and Sam felt as if he'd caressed her. Instantly she felt the need to feel him against her again.

She looked away before she did something extraordinarily stupid.

"If you'd like." At least in the kitchen, she'd have something to keep her hands occupied and her mind busy.

He nodded. "I'll change and be right there," he said, taking the steps two at a time.

He hadn't touched her, but Sam felt as if he had. She watched until he was out of sight, then grinned off into space for a couple of moments before shaking her head and heading for the kitchen. She couldn't wait to hear Charlene's story.

"That was truly amazing. I'll never be able to thank you enough," Sam said to Mac a couple of hours later.

Sam had hunted Mac down and found him in their office after she'd washed the dishes and he'd gone to put Tommy to bed. She shut the door and beamed at him.

"I told you Monica would be a good choice," he said, rising from the desk chair and coming around to her. He brushed back her hair, placed his palm against her neck and brought her closer for a kiss.

"I could get to like meeting with you after dinner," he said huskily when she stepped in as naturally as if they'd been following this routine for years.

"Me, too," she whispered as she kissed him.

A few moments later, he gently released her and went to lean against the desk. "Where do you want to go to dinner on Friday?"

"You choose," she said, walking to the desk and fiddling with one of the pencils there.

"Dancing?"

"Yes, please," she said with a quick smile.

"Then we'll eat at a seafood restaurant I like and move to one of the clubs."

He reached out, as if unable to keep from touching her, capturing her hand in his, his thumb gently rubbing it. "I'm glad Monica liked Charlene's patterns. That's the most likely source of a continuing income."

"That was the most amazing part. The quilts will bring in a lot, but she thinks she can get the patterns published and have ongoing revenue for years. And Alice is going to be a big help. Who would have thought it?"

"Her references *were* great," he said again.

She laughed. "But not in quilting or in knowing someone in the textile industry who might jump-start the process."

"It's always who you know," Mac said. "Looks like your sister is poised for the big time."

Sam nodded, her smile wide. "I'm so happy for her. One of our New Year's resolutions was to try to sell some of her work. Wow, this is it in spades."

"What was another resolution?"

"Get the house repaired."

"Carson stopped by this morning, the contractor I told you about. He'll have some estimates before the end of the week. He seems to think it would be better if he handled the repairs. I don't know why he doubts my ability."

She laughed. "He probably thinks you are too high-tech. Charlene didn't tell me that he'd been by."

"He called me after he left. I guess her later news drove it out of her mind. He says it could be done in a week or so, once the appliances had been ordered and arrive. With Charlene's sales to Monica, you'll have the money to get started right away."

That had also been mentioned at dinner. It was the only downside that Sam could see. If they had money for repairs, she had no reason to continue as a nanny for Tommy. The thought came unbidden.

"What?" he asked, picking up on her change of expression.

"Nothing. Let's wait until everything is signed, sealed and delivered. You know the saying about a bird in the hand."

"Miracles take a little getting used to, is that it?" he asked, swinging their hands back and forth.

"Yes. Did Tommy go to bed all right?"

"He did. Sam, I also got a call from City Works today. The water pipe repairs will be complete tomorrow. Tommy and I can move back home then. I asked Mrs. Horton if she could watch him on Friday evening and she said yes."

"For my thank-you-for-your-hospitality dinner," she said, trying to keep her tone light. Things were spinning out of control. They were leaving. Soon she wouldn't need to have a second job where she saw Tommy or Mac every day.

Which meant she could get on with her schooling and get her degree sooner than expected.

Somehow, the thought didn't excite her as it usually did.

And, if the action plan Monica outlined for her sister came into being, Charlene would start earning money on a regular basis for patterns with extras here and there when one of her quilts sold. That, with her transcription job, would assure plenty of money for repairs.

Nothing would stand in the way of Sam's future.

So why wasn't she happier about the idea?

Charlene knocked on the door. Sam let go Mac's hand and went to answer it.

"Am I interrupting?" she asked.

"Not at all. Mac invited us to dinner on Friday. He told me they are going back home tomorrow and wanted to thank us for having them here."

Charlene looked beyond her sister and smiled at Mac. "Thanks, but I'll pass. Take Sam, though. She doesn't get out much."

Gee, thanks, sis. I need to have the man I'm crazy about think I'm some kind of stay-at-home loser! But Sam didn't voice the comment aloud. "We can go someplace you're comfortable with, Mac said."

"No, actually I came to ask if Tommy could stay here Friday night. Alice said you asked her to watch him and she and I wanted to get started on a new project I have in mind. We'd take good care of him and not begin work until he was in bed."

"Fine with me."

"You could pick him up Saturday morning—maybe come for a pancake breakfast or something," she said, glancing between Sam and Mac.

"Unless you have other plans for Saturday," Sam said, turning halfway around to look at Mac. "You don't have to come by. I could drop Tommy off."

"I'd like a big pancake breakfast," he said, puzzled at Sam's comment. "I'll spell Mrs. Horton by getting home early, letting her come over here and then I'll bring Tommy when I come to pick up Sam."

"Sounds like a plan. Alice just left. I still can't believe all Monica said."

"She's coming again tomorrow, right?" Sam asked.

"Yes, with some preliminary contracts. I'll have to hire an attorney to review them and guard my interests."

Sam smiled at her sister. Charlene might have led a quiet

life these past ten years, but she was smart and would do well in the business end, she predicted.

Mac stood. "I hope it works out extremely well for you."

"I need to do some things before bed," Sam said, using the interruption as an excuse to leave. The McAlhenys were leaving the next day. She'd not leave Mac in the lurch with child care, but if Charlene made as much from the sales as she said at dinner, Sam could soon resume the normal pattern of her life that had been disrupted by Hurricane George.

As she went up to her bedroom, she wondered how long it would take to forget about Mac and Tommy. A very long time—if ever.

The house seemed empty the next evening after Mac and Tommy had left. They'd eaten dinner one more time with the Duncan sisters and then headed for home.

"That Tommy is cute as can be," Charlene said as she sat watching Sam finish the dishes. Mac had offered to help, but she'd sent him off. She was glad for something to do.

"He is," she agreed, smiling as she remembered Tommy telling them something at dinner. He was so serious when explaining things. She just wished she understood him better.

"And his dad's not bad, either," Charlene said slyly.

Sam ignored that and refused to look at her sister. She was trying for a rise out of her and Sam wasn't going to snap at the bait.

"You don't have to work that second job anymore," Charlene said. "I'm so glad after all this time I can do something for you. In fact, if you want, with what Monica thinks I'll bring in this first year, you could quit your job at the Beale Foundation and go to school full-time. You'd have your degree in one more semester if you attend full-time."

Sam turned at that. "Trying to get rid of me?"

Charlene shrugged. "Trying to let you get on with your life—you put it on hold all these years for me and now it's time for you to live it the way you want."

"I've been happy these years, Charlene."

"But I know you want to work out west. Take the opportunity now."

"You need to bank that windfall in case Monica's estimates are a bit inflated," Sam said practically.

"I plan to bank some, but not all. I want to feel I can contribute. Let me do this, Sam."

More than her feelings for Mac were spinning out of control. Sam nodded and wiped down the counters, finished with kitchen chores for the night. "Thank you," she said with a smile.

Later, she commandeered the family computer to check out registration dates for the spring quarter. She had time, if she walked her papers through. Yet the excitement she'd expected to feel just wasn't there. Acting on impulse, she searched for Mac on the computer, and found several articles about his business. And one on the death of his wife. Chris had been a pretty blonde—probably where Tommy got his hair color. Sam stared at the picture of Chris and Mac together for a long time. They looked so in love. Would she ever have a man look at her like that?

She shut down the computer and went up to bed. Her future lay in a different direction than Mac McAlheny and his son and it was time she acted like it.

Friday Sam was ready before Mac arrived. Alice had come straight from the McAlhenys' home and shared a light dinner with Charlene. They were both still in the kitchen talking a mile a minute. Sam listened from the dining room, amused to find out how chatty Alice Horton was once she shed her gruff exterior. She and Charlene were fast becoming best friends. Who would have thought it?

Sam checked her appearance once more in the downstairs mirror when she heard Mac's car. The dress was warm enough for Atlanta's freezing winter nights, but festive enough for any place he chose. Feeling excited as a teenager, she tried deep breaths to calm her nerves.

He knocked and she threw open the door, smiling widely.

The thing about Sam, Mac thought, was he knew where he was with her. Her smile warmed him. Her excitement was refreshing and welcome. The women who he'd seen since Chris died were too self-centered for his own tastes. Too polished and sophisticated. He'd liked being seen with them and they had relished spending time in the limelight, but there was more to life than strutting around to be seen. Sam was genuine and he liked being with her.

He stepped inside, closed the door and wished he could draw her close for a kiss.

"Hi, Sam," Tommy said.

Mac loved his son, but right now, he'd rather he'd run to find Mrs. Horton rather than stay to greet Sam.

"I sleeped in my bed last night," he announced.

"I know you did. We missed you here, though."

"Want to come sleep over at my house?" Tommy asked.

Mac wished he dared second the request.

"Oh, I have my own bedroom right here in this house. Tonight you can sleep over again. Alice and Charlene are in the kitchen, making a special treat—cookies."

Mac scarcely had him out of his jacket before Tommy headed for the kitchen at a run.

"Are you ready? I'll tell Mrs. Horton we're leaving," he said, looking at her and feeling the warmth in his chest. Sam was pretty, but it was her personality that sparkled.

"I'm ready."

He brushed her cheek with the back of his fingers as he passed to go let Mrs. Horton know he was leaving Tommy in her care.

He couldn't wait until it was just he and Sam. She looked fantastic. He wanted her to have a good time tonight. The place he chose was close to the nightclub and once they ate, they'd go dancing. He couldn't wait to hold her in his arms again; it had been too long. And when they were part of an anonymous crowd, it wouldn't matter if he snuck in a kiss or two. No one would know but them.

The ladies in the kitchen had already put Tommy to work adding chocolate chips to the cookie mix. He knew his son was in good hands. Hurrying back to the entryway, he saw Sam standing where he'd left her. Mac smiled as he reached her and swept back her hair from her face and leaned over to kiss her. Her lips were warm and welcoming. His were cool from the freezing outdoor temperature, but she warmed them in a heartbeat.

He could have stood all night kissing Sam, but he wanted more from their evening.

"Ready?" he asked again.

"I sure am," she replied with a wide smile.

The restaurant was crowded. It was Friday night and the spot was popular in Atlanta. The wait was short, however, due to their reservations and soon they were seated at a table for two. The background noise faded as he gazed at her while she studied the menu. She frowned in concentration then glanced up to see his gaze on her.

"What?" she asked.

"Nothing."

"You already know what you want?" she asked.

"I do."

Her.

The thought came unbidden and floored him for a moment. Then he let it settle in. He wanted her—in all the ways a man wanted a woman. Yes, he wanted to take her to bed. But he also wanted to wake up with her. Share meals together. Make plans for the future and do all the mundane chores around the house together.

He was falling in love with Samantha Duncan!

CHAPTER EIGHT

MAC quickly dropped his gaze to the open menu. He knew what he wanted for dinner, but the thought that just crossed his mind had him needing a moment to himself.

He had loved his wife. He mourned her passing every day. How could he be falling in love with someone else? And with someone so different? There were few similarities between Samantha Duncan and Chris. How could he even begin to find another love when Chris had only been dead three years?

The intellectual side of his mind knew life went on. It also knew Chris would have wanted him to be happy. As he would have wished that for her all her life.

But to think of starting life anew with another woman was unthinkable.

Unless it was with Sam.

He looked at her. Her dark hair fell on either side of her face, soft and glossy in the subdued light. He knew how silky it felt. His fingers itched to feel that soft texture again. Faint color highlighted her cheeks. When she looked up, her chocolate-brown eyes held a question. Mac felt like an idiot.

"I think I'll have the scampi," she said, giving him a gentle smile. It kick-started his heart beating out of control.

"Sounds good. I'm having the surf and turf."

"Such a guy thing," she said, wrinkling her nose at him.

He wanted to reach across the table and kiss her. Taking a

deep breath, he deliberately leaned back in his chair and glanced around. Time enough later for that, he hoped.

"Do you come here often?" she asked, closing her menu.

"I've been here once or twice before. Always business meetings. I like the food."

"Do you have many business dinners?" she asked.

He shrugged. "Not often—if I can help it. But if we have out-of-town customers, wives are included and it makes it a better situation all around."

She nodded.

After the waiter had taken their order for dinner, Sam leaned over a bit and said in a conspiratorial voice, "I don't like business dinners."

"Why's that?"

"I find it hard to make small talk with people I don't know. When we have business lunches, it's usually with prospective donors. But dinners have spouses who have no interest in the donation process. Though sometimes they are interested in the services the Beale Foundation provides."

"Our business dinners are to woo customers in placing megaorders with our company. Chris used to love them. I find them a necessary task, but would just as soon have pizza at home with Tommy."

She smiled brightly, but falsely.

Way to go, idiot, he chided himself. Bring Chris up. Was he using her as a defense? Sam had done nothing to make him think she wanted anything beyond what they had—a casual friendship. Granted, she'd been receptive to his kisses, but she hadn't followed up on any of them with suggestions like the women he'd dated over the past couple of years.

In fact, when he thought about it—she had usually spoken of her great dream to move out west and work in a national park. Did that mean she wouldn't be interested in seeing what might develop between them?

It was too early. He still felt floored by the idea of falling

in love again. Tonight was to thank her for her hospitality—
and give her a respite from watching Tommy. He needed
more time to think things through.

There had to be more than physical attraction, though
Sam held that for him in spades. But how much did he
know about her?

"Next weekend Tommy and I are going to see his grandparents in Savannah. Would you like to ride along?" Mac
asked.

Okay, that was changing the subject. "Your parents?" she
asked in surprise.

"Mine and Chris's. What, did you think I didn't have
parents?"

"I guess I didn't really think about it. Ours died so long
ago it seems strange to us to find people with parents and
sometimes grandparents living."

"Both my parents are alive and well and so are Chris's. I
take Tommy to visit every few months—especially at this age.
He's prone to forget people if he doesn't see them frequently."

"I better not," she said slowly. She'd love to see where Mac
grew up. To meet his parents. But she'd feel awkward—especially around Chris's parents. Would they see her as a candidate for their daughter's place in Tommy's life? She
dropped her gaze. She was sure Mac had no intentions along
those lines. They were just—friends.

"Come with us and I'll give you a tour of Savannah while
Tommy is with Jerry and Becca. Those are Chris's parents and
I let him stay there alone part of the weekend so they can spoil
him all they want."

"Must be fun for him."

"He enjoys the visits. Come with us, Sam," he urged.

She longed to go. Would it hurt? "If Charlene is comfortable with me being gone."

"Your sister's really taking off with this quilting thing,
isn't she?" he asked.

"She's in heaven! She loves every aspect. I can't believe how much she's blossomed in the past few days. The accident really changed her from the older sister I remember and now it's as if she's coming back."

"Tell me about her when you were young."

Sam smiled and readily complied. In the telling, she related how happy their family had been, how full of hope and promise. The tragedy of the automobile accident had changed everything—and none of it for the better. But she never complained. He never detected a note of self-pity. She met life head-on and adjusted as the path twisted and turned.

"So now, if she gets some income, maybe it'll be more than enough to support her along with the transcription income she earns."

"And that's a good thing?" Mac knew it was, but wanted Sam's take on it. He was fascinated by the way she thought.

"Yes, for Charlene. It'll mean she's back in charge of her life and won't feel dependent on her younger sister. And, once the repairs are completed and paid for, I can get back to my original plans."

"Ah, the great scheme of moving west."

She smiled and nodded. "I can't wait!"

Mac felt as if he'd been kicked. He didn't want her to move west, or anywhere. Unless it was into his home.

"There are national parks in the east as well," he said easily.

"Sure. But I've lived here all my life. The west is so different. Wide-open spaces, different wildlife, mountains. So much to see, to learn. It's been my dream since I was fifteen."

"We have the Appalachians."

"Foothills compared to the Rockies or the Sierras. I want to see it all, be a part of it. Spread my wings and fly."

He nodded, hoping he gave nothing away. Her passion for her goal wasn't what he wanted to hear. He couldn't move his business or his home. He had a son to raise. He wanted him near his grandparents. Mac wanted Sam to be a part of his life, not try to find a way to fit into the future she looked for so hungrily. Was that selfish of him?

When their food was served, Mac deliberately changed the subject, hoping to find common ground. They discussed movies they liked. No common ground there. She liked chick flicks and he preferred action-adventure epics. When they discussed books, he wasn't surprised to hear that she avidly read everything she could about the American west—history, geology, Native American cultures. His favorites were mysteries where he could try to figure out the ending before it was revealed.

Food was one area they had in common, both liking seafood, Italian and rich desserts.

They talked through dinner, through dessert and beyond. It was late when he realized the restaurant was practically empty and he and Sam had been talking for hours. It had only seemed like minutes.

She glanced around at his look. "Gracious, are we almost the last? What time is it?"

"Close to eleven."

"I've had such fun," she said, smiling at him.

Mac caught his breath at the feelings that cascaded through him at the sight of her smile. Her delight with the evening was clearly evident. He could go on forever.

"Ready to leave? We can still go dancing."

"Maybe not. If you wouldn't mind, I'd like to call it an evening. You could come in when we get home and have a nightcap or something."

Disappointed he wouldn't get to hold her, dance with her as they had on New Year's Eve, he nonetheless welcomed the invitation.

But they were not alone when they entered the house. Charlene and Alice were together in the dining room, with papers spread all over and different quilts folded nearby.

"We got Tommy to bed at eight. He went right to sleep," Alice reported.

"We're hard at it now, so if you two won't mind, we won't join you. It's late and we want to wrap up soon," Charlene said.

"No, we were just going to have something to drink," Sam said, bemused by this side of her sister.

She and Mac entered the kitchen.

"What'll it be?" she asked.

"Hot chocolate. It's too late for coffee if I want to sleep tonight."

"Want to stay over? Seems a shame to wake Tommy now. He's fine here."

"I'll go home and come back in the morning to get him."

"For pancake breakfast," she said, already gathering the ingredients for the hot beverage.

Mac leaned against the counter, out of her way. He could watch her all day and night and still wish he had more time. Odd, he'd never noticeably felt that way about Chris. Of course, he'd known her most of his life. He'd loved her for years. But there was something special about Samantha Duncan that captivated him in ways he hadn't known before.

Conscious of the two women in the adjacent room, Mac kept their meeting brief. He finished his cup of hot chocolate as soon as it was cool enough to drink.

"I'll be by in the morning around nine," he said, brushing her lips with his and then leaving.

Sam stared after him, hearing him bid Alice and Charlene good-night. She had expected something more. But how awkward would a full-blown kiss have been with her sister ten steps away. Or worse, if she'd come into the kitchen for something.

Sighing gently, she ran water in the cups and began to plan for tomorrow's breakfast. She'd see him again in a few short hours. Remembering all they'd talked about during the evening, she went up to bed in a happy frame of mind.

* * *

Sam was wakened in the morning when Tommy knocked on her door. Entering when bidden, he ran to her bed.

"Time for pancakes," he said, smiling at her.

What a great way to wake up. She smiled back, delighted in his innocent excitement.

"It just about is. How about I get dressed, get you dressed and we'll go make the batter?" she asked. He loved helping.

"'Kay."

In less than twenty minutes the two of them were in the kitchen pulling out bowls, mixing utensils and ingredients.

She didn't let him near the hot stove, but had him happily standing on a stool stirring the batter—thankfully only spilling a little. A small price to pay for his obvious happiness. She watched him, her heart swelling with love. He was a precious child. It was fun to see life through the eyes of a child. It made everything seem wondrous and new again.

She was turning sausages in the skillet when she heard the knock on the front door.

"I bet that's your daddy," she said to Tommy. Lifting him down, she turned off the stove and followed at a slower pace when he ran to the front door. The heavy knob was too much for him, so she knew he couldn't open the door before she got there.

Checking, she saw it was Mac and swung the door open.

He smiled at her and reached down to take his son up in his arms. "Hey, sport. How are you doing?"

"We making pancakes," Tommy said proudly, struggling to get down. He ran back to the kitchen.

"Making pancakes or a mess?"

"Some of each. Come on back, I have sausages on the stove and don't want him in there alone." She hurried back, feeling flustered and excited at the same time. She was glad she'd taken time to dress first thing and apply a tiny bit of makeup. The slim jeans and sweater fit perfectly and she hoped he noticed.

"What can I do?" Mac asked when he followed her into the kitchen.

"Set the table?" she suggested, keeping an eye on Tommy. In a few moments, Charlene came in.

"Coffee," she said dramatically. "I may fall asleep right now if I don't get some soon."

Sam laughed. She felt bubbling with happiness. Pouring her sister a cup, she handed it over. "Don't want you falling asleep now, you might tumble to the floor. How late were you up?"

"Far too late." Charlene sipped the coffee. "Ah, ambrosia."

Mac had poured himself a cup and refilled hers. It was so domestic. As if they were choreographed.

"It was after one when Alice left. Then I was so keyed up, I couldn't get to sleep right away," Charlene said after taking another swallow of coffee.

"You should have slept in later," Sam said.

"Can't. Monica is coming over this morning and taking me to her shop. She wants my help displaying the quilts she's selling. And to see where she would let us offer classes. Alice is meeting me there."

"Cool. Maybe I'll tag along," Sam said.

"If you like. Otherwise, wait until we have it all set up and come in as a customer and give us your honest opinion."

"I'd like to see it, too," Mac said. "Maybe Sam and I can both come later. After lunch? Does that give you enough time to set up the display?"

"Perfect," Charlene said.

Sam sped up the breakfast, making Charlene the first pancakes, then some for Tommy. Sitting around the table, she was conscious of Mac sitting only a few inches away. His and hers were finished at the same time and she enjoyed the meal more than any she'd had recently. Unless it was the one from last night. Or the Black and White Ball. Okay, so any meal with Mac had been special!

* * *

When Charlene left, Mac offered to help with the dishes.

"No need. I can get them done quickly."

"Then I'm calling Carson. He said he'd have estimated cost for the repair work here. Maybe we can get you started on that."

"It would be wonderful, but you must have other plans for Saturday."

"Not this weekend. I told Charlene I'd bring you by after lunch. You're stuck with me until then."

She smiled; being stuck with him was not how she viewed it.

The trip to Monica's shop turned out to be fun. The storefront was larger than Sam expected—huge glass windows display-ing completed quilts, crocheted sweaters and baby sets and knitted afghans. Plus displays of patterns, cross-stitch and skeins of brightly colored yarn.

The inside was also spacious, but with a warm and cozy feel. They wandered through—just like a customer might. Mac carried Tommy, lest he dash around and get into mischief. He walked beside Sam.

"Hello," one of the salesclerks greeted them. She smiled at Tommy. "Your son is adorable."

Sam blinked. Did the young woman think Tommy was hers? She opened her mouth to tell her he wasn't, but closed it and merely smiled. She couldn't blame her for mistaking the image they must give. Strangers would think they were a family. For a moment she felt a pang. Would she one day find a man who would love her, want to share her life? Someone she'd love?

It would have to be when she was established as a park ranger. She wouldn't find someone like that in Atlanta. That would tie her down when she felt the future was just opening up.

Except for Mac, something inside whispered. He would never tie her down.

But that would never work. Her dreams lay elsewhere. And he was still connected to his wife even though she was long dead.

Feeling a bit let down with the thought, she looked for Charlene. She saw Alice first.

After complimenting them on the display, hearing about the classes offered and watching as two women who were listening immediately signed up, Sam was content when Mac asked if she were ready to leave. This was Charlene's world now. And Sam was happy to see how well her sister interacted. She'd love teaching quilting and she was already happier than Sam had ever seen her.

"Yes," Sam said.

"Let's take Tommy to the park. There's enough snow still for him to try making a snowman," Mac said.

"I'd like that."

She had other things she could do, but Sam relished every moment she could spend with Mac. And soon enough there'd be no reason.

When Sam arrived at Mac's home on Monday after work, Alice waited, giving her a brief rundown on Tommy's day and then headed out for the class she taught. Sam had hardly begun dinner when Mac entered.

"I didn't expect you so early," she said.

"I wanted to have one of your home-cooked meals," he said.

The kitchen seemed instantly cozier, she thought. Tommy played with toys in the area farthest away from the cooking. He greeted his dad, then returned to the make-believe world he'd created.

It seemed natural for Sam to ask how Mac's day had been. He then asked about hers and the evening took on an even more surreal feeling. She remembered her mother and father talking together in the evenings, sharing the parts of their lives that were spent away from each other. Enjoying just being together.

As she did with Mac.

For the short time she had left.

Soon she wouldn't have to work for the extra money. But she didn't want to think about that yet.

Each evening during the week Mac arrived home earlier than expected. Whenever Sam suggested leaving, he'd always ask her to stay until Tommy was in bed. A ritual developed with them reading to Tommy and then both tucking him in beneath the covers. Mac would then offer her a cup of tea or something so she stayed even later. Each night ended in a kiss. Sometimes Sam wanted to leave earlier just to get her kiss earlier. But she reveled in every moment together.

Thursday he surprised her again. "I asked Mrs. Horton to watch Tommy tomorrow. Same deal as last week. She and Charlene are meeting in the evening, so he was invited to your home again."

"With pancakes for breakfast Saturday?" she asked.

He nodded. "Or we can eat somewhere on the road to Savannah."

"Let's eat at home. Then if anything gets spilled, we can clean him up before we leave."

"I like the way you think."

"Do your parents know I'm coming?" Suddenly Sam wondered if this was a wise move. They wouldn't read anything into their relationship, would they? It wasn't as if he were taking her home to meet the parents, so to speak. Merely to show her Savannah while Tommy was with his maternal grandparents.

"I mentioned I was bringing you. Is that a problem?"

"No, they probably want to know Tommy's caregiver," she said, trying to be practical.

"I think of you as more than that," Mac said quietly.

"Tomorrow night we'll eat a quick bite and then definitely go dancing."

Sam liked the way he said that, as if he would not take no for an answer. As if she'd give one. Dancing with him at the Black and White Ball had been thrilling. She couldn't wait to repeat the experience.

She wore a new dress to dinner. One that had a flaring skirt that would allow her to dance slow, fast and in between. The rich burgundy color made her look her best.

Mac took her to an Italian restaurant.

"You remembered how much I love Italian," she said. Their conversation last week had encompassed all kinds of information exchanges.

"We're not going to talk all night this time," he said as he followed her to the table.

"Because we'd miss the dancing," she said with a laugh. Feeling almost giddy as she sat opposite him, she pulled out the menu and glanced through it. Taking a deep breath, she loved the aromas that filled her senses. She peeked at him and found his gaze on her.

"I'll have the ravioli," she said.

He signaled the waiter and gave their order.

Sam was brimming with news. She beamed at him. "I may have just the nanny for you. Someone who can live in. That way you wouldn't have to juggle schedules between Mrs. Horton and me, but have someone there all the time. She came into the office earlier this week looking for a live-in position. We've done a reference check and everything is perfect. She's very capable, energetic and loves children. She worked for several years in a preschool in Augusta and moved to Atlanta after her husband died to be near their only daughter who's going to Georgia State."

"Someone from the Foundation?" he asked. Mac knew there would be changes with Charlene now contributing to the family income. But he didn't expect Sam to talk about leaving so soon.

"Yes. She's almost deaf, can only hear a few sounds. But in watching children, she doesn't turn her back."

"I don't think so. I need someone who can deal with a rambunctious three-year-old. Too much could go wrong with someone who can't hear." He appreciated her offer. But he wanted Sam in their lives. For as long as she'd stay.

"She has a service dog—he's her ears." Sam leaned forward. "Donations are great, the Foundation needs every penny we get, but even more, we need people to be willing to hire qualified employees who may have a slight disadvantage. I would never recommend anyone who would cause a risk to another—especially to a child. Would you at least interview her?"

"Let me think about it," he said. He didn't like the way this conversation was going.

"I think it would easier for Tommy when I stop watching him to move into a permanent nanny. And I think Mrs. Horton might find a new direction if she continues to work with Charlene on this quilting business."

"I said I'd think about it."

Sam nodded, sitting back, her expression resigned. Mac felt a twinge of guilt. He couldn't consider someone else watching Tommy when he wanted Sam there full-time.

Sam felt let down. She doubted he'd even give Kristin a chance. She knew the situation could end up a perfect solution for all concerned. What little boy wouldn't love to be around a dog, one so well trained as Buddy. And Kristin loved to cook and bake. She'd brought enough batches of cookies and treats into the office that Sam could give a testimonial. And her own daughter was proof of how well she watched children. Kristin had hated to give up her position at the day care center in Augusta, but wanted to be closer to her daughter.

But the age-old concern about disabilities always rose.

Mac reached out and caught her hand in his, squeezing slightly. "I meant it, I'll give it some serious consideration. Maybe you can arrange an interview. I'm not making any promises, but I will interview her, see what she can do. I want harmony in my household, someone for Tommy to like."

She was afraid to hope, but she'd take what she could get. "I'll see what I can arrange."

"But if I think it would in any way endanger my child, no, I won't consider it."

"Neither would I," she said, wondering if her real goal was to find Kristin a position, or find a reason to continue contact with Mac. Her hand tingled from his grip, and her attention was on Mac, not the possibility of finding a perfect match for one of their registrants. She hoped it was because she wanted the best for the older woman. But it wouldn't hurt to have an ongoing connection with the man opposite her after her stint as child care provider was over.

The waiter arrived with their salad. Sam hated to have Mac release her hand. She wished they could have held hands throughout dinner.

She had it bad. And instead of saying something scintillating and enthralling, she had to talk about his hiring someone else to watch Tommy.

She resolved right then that the rest of the night was going to be for them, no talk about Charlene or Tommy and especially not Chris.

They discussed what time they would leave in the morning, what to see first in the historic city on the Georgia coast. Sam told him of a documentary film she'd seen recently and they discussed likes and dislikes of documentary filmmakers.

When they finished eating, Mac called for the check and they were soon on their way. In less than ten minutes they entered the nightclub and immediately felt the rhythm of the music. They were shown to a table near the dance floor, drink orders taken, and as soon as the waitress left, Mac rose and asked Sam to dance.

The pace was fast and fun. She moved with the beat and was delighted to note what a good dancer Mac was. This evening would prove fun on all fronts.

They danced the next one as well, stopping to take a quick break when Mac saw their beverages on the minuscule table.

"I love dancing," Sam said, draining her sparkling water. She was warm from all the exercise, but having a terrific time.

"We'll have to do it often," he replied, his eyes on her.

A slow song started and Mac rose again. "This is why I came," he murmured, pulling her out onto the floor and folding her into his embrace. She snuggled up against him. She was glad he wanted to dance so close. Her forehead rested against his jaw. Partway through the song, he turned his head to give her a kiss. She looked up and he lowered his face to kiss her on the lips.

Smiling against his mouth, she returned the kiss. Tonight was as magical as the Black and White Ball had been. Only better. She wasn't worried about someone finding out how she came. Tonight, she'd been invited.

The evening continued in a like manner until closing time. They danced almost every dance. Sam especially loved the slow ones. Conversation was difficult, but she didn't mind. Mac held her as if she were precious and important to him.

Finally the last call for drinks was given.

"Oh, I didn't realize it was so late," she said, looking at Mac's watch. It was well after midnight.

"Ready to leave?" he asked.

"No, I'm having too much fun, but all good things come to an end," she said, picking up her purse. "Let me make a quick stop and I'll be ready to leave."

"Not ducking out like last time," he said.

She looked puzzled then laughed. "No. I'll be right back."

The drive home through the darkened streets almost put Sam to sleep. She was pleasantly tired. She hated to end their night together, but Mac was a father who had to be up early in the morning. And she had planned to be up early, too. Tommy would be in to see to that.

Mac walked Sam to the door reluctant to say good-night. But it was late and he needed some time to come to terms with his feelings for her. It felt wrong to leave her at the door. He wanted her to belong with him. To share his life. Help him raise Tommy, and maybe have a few children of their own. Some sweet little girl with her mother's big brown eyes, and her delightful laugh. Or another son or two.

When he entered his home a short time later, he looked at it as he imagined she must see it. He'd bought the house after Chris died. They'd struggled so hard to get the business established, forgoing all but the basics until it took off. By the time it had, she hadn't been there to enjoy the fruits of their labor.

Did Sam know that? Did she like the way the house was decorated or wish to change things? His mother had decorated it. He wouldn't care if Sam changed everything except Tommy's room, if she'd agree to marry him.

Marriage!

He went through to the living room and sat on the sofa, the lights off. Leaning against the cushions, he let his mind wander in the dark. He realized he really did want to marry her. He never thought he would go that route again. The agony of losing Chris had been almost unbearable. If he hadn't had Tommy to care for, he wasn't sure he would have made it. Could he open himself up to the possibility of such terrible loss again?

What choice did he have? Risk everything to savor every moment spent together, or part now and feel as if he was losing an arm or a leg—or having a large part of his heart ripped out.

Even knowing the devastating pain that could be waiting, he'd choose to spend whatever time they had together. With any luck, they'd have another fifty or sixty years together. He couldn't risk not spending those years with Sam. How bleak life would be if she wasn't a part of it.

He'd ask her tomorrow to marry him. They could shop for a ring together in Savannah, and then he could introduce her to his parents as his future wife. Tommy already loved her. They would, too, in short order. Just as he did.

Already impatient for the morning, Mac rose and went to bed. He'd probably not sleep, but the sooner the night hours passed, the sooner he could ask Sam to be his wife.

Sam wished she could have slept in late on Saturday, but she only lingered in bed a short time after she heard Tommy. Rising, she went to peep in his room, but the bed was empty. She heard Charlene's voice, so knew Tommy would be fine while she took a quick shower to wake up.

She'd had such a marvelous time last evening. Remembering their dancing as she showered, she couldn't keep the silly smile from her face. It had been so special. And she had all weekend with Mac. She could hardly wait. She'd only been to Savannah once. It was a charming city and she'd get an insider's view with Mac giving her the tour.

When she entered the kitchen after dressing, Charlene already had bacon frying and Tommy was mixing the pancake batter like last week, spilling a bit over the edge of the bowl every couple of swirls of the spoon. He was having a grand time and it was obvious Charlene was, too.

"Good morning," Sam said, heading for the coffeepot. This weekend it was she who needed a huge jolt of caffeine.

"Hi. Did you have fun last night? I tried to wait up, but by eleven-thirty I was too tired."

"I didn't get home until way after two. Good thing you didn't wait up."

"I making pancakes," Tommy said proudly.

"So you are," Sam said, walking over to give him a quick kiss on his cheek. "Looks good." She glanced at her sister. "Thanks for watching him while I dressed."

"He's no trouble. We had fun last night. Alice and I popped popcorn and then we all watched a Disney movie. He was out like a light before it ended."

"Then you and Alice talked more about your quilts?"

"Yes. We are excited about our classes—they start next weekend. And we'll have one on Wednesday nights. With her background in teaching adult education, she's given me lots of great ideas. I can't believe all this. Sometimes I think I'm dreaming."

"So Alice would participate?" Sam asked.

Charlene nodded. "With the Saturday classes. Maybe Wednesdays, too, after next semester when her teaching assignment is up."

"Or if you have daytime classes, I think I have a replacement for her with Mac. If he likes Kristin, Alice and I could both be out of a job. Kristin would live in. I hated to take Alice's job away, but Mac really wanted a live-in housekeeper cum nanny."

"She knew the job was temporary. She'll be as excited about this as I am," Charlene said.

Sam sipped her coffee, delighting in the change in her sister. Nothing was mentioned about feeling awkward going out in public in the wheelchair. Not that she should feel that way, but for years, she'd scarcely left the house. It was only recently she'd started making friends in her quilting guild. Now this. Sam was amazed. And gave full credit to Mac for bringing Monica into the mix and making it happen.

When the doorbell sounded, Sam's heart skipped a beat. She put down the cup.

"I'll get it," she said, trying to sound normal. But her heart rate soared as she hurried to the door.

Mac grinned when he saw her. He stepped inside, closed the door and pulled her into his arms for a long kiss. His face was cold, but that thought lasted only a second before the deep feelings she experienced each time he kissed her took over.

When they broke, she was breathing hard. She had missed him since seeing him a few hours earlier.

"Sleep well?" he asked, taking off his jacket.

He was wearing a dark sweater and dark pants. He looked enticing, dangerous and oh so sexy.

"Slept well, if not long. You?"

"No, I missed you."

She blinked. "Really?"

He glanced into the dining room.

"Are Charlene and Tommy around?" he asked.

"They're in the kitchen. Tommy's helping with the pancakes. You don't want to stand too close—the batter is being spread liberally all around."

"That's my kid."

Mac reached for Sam's hand.

"Come on, we have coffee all ready," Sam said.

"Wait a minute," he said. "I have something to ask you. I know we haven't known each other for long. But it feels longer. You know what I mean?"

She nodded. She felt that way each time she saw him.

"And we get along together. Tommy is crazy about you, and you've been wonderful with him."

She smiled, pleased Tommy liked her so much and that she was able to take care of a child when she had no experience doing so before.

"Samantha Duncan, would you marry me?" he asked in a rush.

CHAPTER NINE

SAM stared at him. Had she heard him correctly? He wanted to *marry* her?

For a moment her mind was paralyzed. She couldn't think, couldn't speak. Blood pounded through her, making a roaring in her ears. He had not asked her...*he had not!*

Then she shook her head and pulled her hand free, stepping back two steps, feeling the shock through every inch. She had never expected this. What had he said? That Tommy was crazy about her. That she and Mac were good together?

"I can't marry you." Her dream of living in the west flashed into mind. She clutched it desperately. She'd been planning to go west for almost half her life. Suddenly Chad's face appeared in her mind. He'd let her down so badly. Could she trust in Mac? She wanted marriage—someday. But after she'd done what she wanted with her life. Not put it on hold again like she'd had to do when Charlene needed her.

Panic made her blurt out, "I'm leaving Atlanta. For the first time since my parents died, I don't have to be responsible for Charlene. I can't get burdened with a child, someone who would need care for years to come. I'll be an old lady by the time I get to finally do what I want. That's not fair to ask me. I can't marry you. I can't!"

Instantly she wished she could recall the words. Make them sound different. Tommy was a delightful child but he was young and needed parents to raise him for the next decade and beyond. She felt her heart race. This wasn't what she had expected when she opened the door. For a moment she felt resentful that Mac had changed everything.

Mac's expression closed. He stared at her impassively. He could have been a stranger.

"I apologize if I threw you into a panic. I misread the situation," he said stiffly.

Sam felt as if she were standing in quicksand. Everything was shifting. "I thought you wouldn't ever marry again. You said that once. I haven't led you on, have I? I mean, I like being with you and with Tommy. But I can't get married before I have a chance to do what I've wanted to do most of my life. Don't you see? When would I have time for me? I can't marry anyone!"

"I understand." His voice was cool, his expression still closed.

She was in full panic mode. Yet she noticed his change—as if the lights had gone out of his eyes. It was frightening to see him so reserved and controlled. But he'd shocked her. She hadn't expected a proposal from him.

"I told you about wanting to be a ranger," she explained, trying to sound reasonable. She felt as if she'd explode. Her skin felt too tight to contain her. Her heart pounded. How could he ask her? He knew she had plans, goals that finally looked as if they were within reach. He wanted to change everything. How could he ask her to choose?

"You did," he acknowledged.

"Didn't you believe me?" she asked, wondering what she could have done differently. She hadn't meant to lead him on. These last few weeks had been delightful but they hadn't altered her life's goals. She loved spending time with Mac, but she had never thought it would lead to this!

"I do believe you. I thought—never mind what I thought. Let's forget I ever said anything," he said.

"Oh, Mac, I won't ever forget. Thank you. I…if things…

I don't know." She turned and ran up the stairs. Already regretting her words about Tommy being a burden, she couldn't tell him he'd ruined everything. Why couldn't they have just continued as friends? He meant more to her than anyone she'd ever known. But she was wary of commitment—thanks in large part to Chad. But the past couldn't be changed and the future she'd always dreamed about was finally in sight. Mac wanted her to give up her dream and stay in Atlanta.

Entering her room, she closed the door quietly and paced for a moment, her energy levels off the charts. Her nerves were shot. How could he? Going to the window, Sam stared out not seeing a thing. *Friends,* that's what she wanted. How could he have misconstrued that?

Closing her eyes, she could almost feel his arms come around her. Feel how alive she felt when she was in them. Opening them again, she glanced around at the posters that filled her wall. Mesa Verde, Grand Canyon, Arches. She wanted so much to be part of that. She couldn't tie herself down to Atlanta for the rest of her life.

Yet she felt as if a part of her had just died.

What now? Did they continue with her watching Tommy until he decided if Kristin would suit? It wouldn't be fair to him if he loved her. To have her around every night.

But wait—he hadn't said anything about love.

She frowned, replaying his words in her mind. There had been nothing about undying passion for her. About finding her so irresistible he couldn't live without her. About loving her as much as he'd loved Chris.

Suddenly she realized what had happened. She'd recommended Kristin for the live-in position last night and somewhere along the line Mac had decided Sam would make a better live-in nanny. If they were married, she'd be home most evenings and they'd only need a daytime housekeeper. Much easier to find a daily when Alice Horton left.

Leaning her forehead against the cold windowpane, she let

the sadness wash through her as the panic gradually faded. If she wanted to stay in Atlanta, never getting to try the ranger job, she could not ask for a better man to make a life with. Mac was caring for his son. Had suffered a terrible blow yet managed to move on and make a good home for Tommy. He was wildly successful in business and seemed to have lots of friends.

A life with him would be easy and fun.

But not without love. She couldn't imagine marrying anyone who didn't adore her. There were too many ups and downs in life to go through it with someone who only wanted her to watch his son.

Tommy is crazy about you.

"Oh, Mac, why couldn't *you* be crazy about me?" she said softly.

Sam didn't know how long she gazed out the window, the churning emotions and jumbled thoughts making time fly; or stand still. How would she ever face him again? Her heart ached. These last few weeks had been wonderful, exciting, different. But he'd changed everything with his proposal. And she wasn't sure she could work for him anymore.

She had to introduce him to Kristin immediately and hope they clicked. If so, she'd be able to make plans for her final classes at college. Move forward toward her goal.

Her intercom sounded. They'd installed it right after the accident in case Charlene ever needed her in the night.

"Sam, can I talk to you?" her sister asked.

She didn't want to talk to anyone. She didn't want to move. His words echoed over and over in her mind. And her rationale strengthened with every heartbeat.

"Mac and Tommy are gone. Please come down," Charlene said.

She crossed to the speaker and pressed the button. She had never refused when her sister needed her.

"I'll be right there."

"What's going on?" Charlene asked when Sam reached the stairs. "Mac came into the kitchen and said he had to take Tommy home. Before he even had his pancakes. That didn't sit too well with Master Tommy, I can tell you. What happened?"

"He asked me to marry him," Sam said slowly as she descended the stairs.

"He did?" Charlene's face lit up. "How wonderful! I didn't know how to bring up future plans when you've done so much for me and all. But Alice and I have been talking about her moving in. She wasn't sure if you'd approve, but if you're getting married, that'll work out fine. You won't have to worry about me. Alice said she'd help whenever I need it. And she and I are going to be so involved with the…" Charlene trailed off, studying Sam's expression. "What?"

"I turned him down," Sam said, sinking down on the third step.

Charlene looked puzzled. She rolled her chair to the foot of the steps.

"Why ever in the world did you do that? Don't you love him?"

Sam went still. She *liked* Mac, a great deal. She enjoyed being with him. Despite his wealth, he wasn't arrogant or overbearing, but fun to be with. His kisses were like magic, making her feel special and cherished. She rubbed her chest where her heart ached inside it. Did she more than like him?

Stopping the directions of those thoughts, she avoided her sister's gaze. She was not going to fall in love with Mac. She was *not!*

"The timing for marriage isn't right. I want to be a park ranger."

"Is the one mutually exclusive of the other?" Charlene asked.

"It is if he only wants to marry me to get a nanny for Tommy."

Charlene looked surprised at that. "That was his reason for proposing?"

Sam nodded. She met Charlene's gaze. "I'm glad you'll have someone to watch out for you. I'm going to see about applying for a final full-time semester at college like you suggested." The decision was easy when everything fell into place. Charlene would have enough help to stay in the house with Sam gone. And with her job and the extra income from quilting, she'd have more than enough money to support herself.

Kristin would make the perfect nanny for Tommy.

And Sam would have the job she'd always dreamed about.

Somehow she expected to feel happier about everything.

"That surprises me," Charlene said. "It sounded so romantic, meeting at the ball, him tracking you down. Almost like Cinderella."

"Which makes you the mean stepsister," Sam said, not willing to see anything good about the situation. Romance was overrated. She'd discovered that ten years ago. "Besides, by tracking me down, he got me fired from my job."

"And gave you a better one with more pay."

Sam nodded. There was little to fault with Mac. And a lot to admire.

"I'll miss Tommy," Charlene said wistfully. "He's so cute. But I guess that's the way of things." She turned and rolled her chair into the dining room.

Sam sat in gloomy silence for a couple of minutes. She'd miss Tommy, too. He was an enchanting child. She'd miss his father even more. Feeling as old as the mountains she planned to explore, she rose and went to their study to use the computer. She'd check out class schedules, and maybe look at job opportunities at some of the parks she wanted to see.

Mac drove home only halfway listening to Tommy's chatter. He felt numb. After Chris died, he'd never expected to find another woman he would want to spend his life with. Irony struck. For the past couple of years he'd been considered a prime marriage candidate. Now the one woman he wanted didn't want him. Wouldn't his ex-girlfriends love to hear that?

He glanced in the rearview mirror at his son. Tommy was quietly babbling to the little car he held in his hand. For a moment, Mac's heart clutched. Sam had called him a burden. How could anyone think this precious child was not worth the effort to raise him? He'd been fooled. He'd thought the attention Sam gave his son was genuine. He didn't realize it was just part of her job. That she was friendly with everyone and he was no exception.

He had said he'd interview the woman she was recommending, but now he wasn't sure. Maybe it would be better to sever all ties with Sam immediately. Seeing her, knowing she didn't care for him, would only hurt.

Not as much as losing Chris had, but pretty close. At least Sam was alive and soon to be happy doing what she wanted. He wanted to be glad for that. But he could only see the gaping hole her leaving would make in his life.

"Pancakes?" Tommy asked when they reached home. Mac hadn't waited to see if Sam would come back downstairs. There was nothing else to say. He'd bid Charlene goodbye and brought Tommy home. Now it was up to him to fix pancakes. How he wished his own disappointment could be resolved so easily.

Once they finished eating, Mac put Tommy in his car seat and began the drive to Savannah. He'd thought Sam would be with him. He'd even mentioned to his mother that he'd be bringing someone home with him. He had hoped this last week that it would be as his fiancée. Instead she wasn't even accompanying them. The weekend loomed long and lonely.

Monday morning Sam contacted Kristin about interviewing with Mac. The woman was delighted for the opportunity. Sam made arrangements for her to be at Mac's office at ten and then called Mac's secretary to confirm the time. He had obviously told her about the interview as she was expecting Sam's call.

"Will you be accompanying Ms. Wilson?" she asked.

"No, Kristin can manage on her own. It will give them a chance to speak candidly and help Mac see how competent she is." She longed to see him. She'd been miserable all weekend. At a loose end since the trip to Savannah hadn't materialized for her, she tried to fill the hours with information on the western parks. But their final conversation echoed in her mind, distracting her. She was very ashamed of the way she'd turned down his offer. It had been due to shock, but that was no excuse.

Even if he didn't love her, he had offered to marry her. She should have been kinder in her refusal.

"And will you be at the house when Mrs. Horton leaves tonight?" the secretary asked.

Obviously Mac had told her the entire story.

"Of course. Until he hires a replacement." She would keep up her commitments no matter what. But she knew it would never be the same. If he arrived home before Tommy's bedtime, she'd have to leave instantly. No more friendly meals. No evenings spent together talking over everything under the sun.

No good-night kisses.

She hung up the phone and tried to capture some of the enthusiasm for her future job. The anticipation she expected when it was finally within reach was dampened by the memory of Mac's face when she'd crudely refused his offer of marriage. She needed to apologize for that. She should have been more gracious. But he'd caught her by surprise.

When Sam arrived at Mac's at six, she saw an unknown car in the driveway. It wasn't Mac's or Alice Horton's. Hurrying in from the cold, she opened the back door and saw Kristin at the stove and her service dog, Buddy, lying nearby, watching Tommy. The little boy had several trucks scattered around and was playing some game with them.

Alice sat at the table. She nodded at Sam when she entered. Kristin Wilson turned and gave her a bright smile. "I may have the job," she said in her monotonal voice. She smiled at Tommy and looked back at the stew she was preparing.

"Mr. McAlheny brought Mrs. Wilson over this morning to see how she got along with Tommy. I've been helping and, for the most part, observing. I think they'll get along fine. That dog nudges her anytime there's any sound—like Tommy asking something. She's already taught him the sign for milk and cookies."

"Great." Sam's heart sank. It looked as if her connection with Mac and Tommy was ending even earlier than she thought.

"I can wait until tomorrow to give Mr. McAlheny my report. Or you can tell him when he gets here. Mrs. Wilson should get to know Tommy's bedtime routine as well."

"I'll stay until Mac gets home," Sam said, shedding her coat and laying it across the back of one of the chairs.

Once Alice had left, Sam crossed over to Kristin.

"How are things?" she asked, facing the other woman so she could see her lips.

"I think fine. The little boy is well mannered. I expect there will be times when he has a hissy fit, but I can manage. Buddy will warn me about any sounds. And I can hear a high-pitched scream. I heard enough of the children at the day care center."

"Something smells wonderful," Sam said, peering at the pot on the stove.

"A stew. It's simmered all afternoon."

Kristin Wilson could talk in a monotone. She didn't hear her own voice, but had perfected the ability to communicate in a hearing world.

"This is a beautiful home," she said, watching Tommy. "It would be a wonderful job if I get it. And not far from the college. Mr. McAlheny even said my daughter, Sarah, could stay over when she wanted. I can't thank you enough for recommending me."

"I'm happy it's going to work out." Sam was happy for Kristin. It was her own selfish self that wanted to hold back the inevitable.

Tommy came over and looked at the two women. He then went and leaned against Kristin's leg. "I'm hungry."

"Dinner ready soon. Want to wash your hands?"

He nodded. Kristin picked him up and took him to the powder room in the hall. Sam watched, feeling another pang. Just last Friday Tommy would have run to her. Now he was already switching his allegiance.

Isn't that what she wanted? She would feel terrible if he had separation anxiety when she left. He'd been very attached to Louise and still missed her.

That obviously wouldn't be a problem with her departure.

Sam heard Mac's car. Her heart sped up. Kristin and Tommy were still down the hall. She'd greet him alone.

Jumping to her feet, she considered running out the front door when he came in the back, but that was a chicken way to act. She'd done nothing wrong—except in the way she'd refused his offer of marriage. She owed him an apology for that.

He opened the door and stopped a moment when he saw her. Coming inside, he closed the door, his gaze moving around the kitchen. "I see Mrs. Horton's car is gone. But Kristin's is still here."

"Yes. Alice said she does well with Tommy. And apparently Tommy loves her dog. I knew he would."

"Where are they?" he asked as he took off his jacket and put it across the chair next to the one where Sam had laid hers.

"Washing up for dinner."

"Something does smell wonderful," he commented.

"Alice said she'd give you her full report in the morning,

but I could tell you she thinks Kristin will be perfect. Tommy already goes to her."

He inclined his head in a half nod. "I was impressed when we met this morning. I called all her references this afternoon and haven't heard a single negative word about her or her work."

"Great. I thought she'd work or I wouldn't have recommended her. She's terrific with children and loves working with them."

Mac reached into his suit coat inner pocket and withdrew an envelope. "In anticipation of a good report, I drew up a final check. I'll be sure to be home early until Kristin gets settled in. We won't need you to come by anymore." He handed her the envelope.

Sam blinked. She knew she wasn't needed, but it felt like a blow to hear him say not to come again. She gave a valiant smile. "I know Tommy will be in good hands."

"I hope he won't be a burden to Kristin."

"Mac, I'm so sorry. It was thoughtless and wrong of me to say that. He's adorable and I'll really miss him." She wanted to say more, but the words wouldn't come.

Mac didn't say anything. He studied the stove, avoiding Sam's eyes. She put on her coat. "I'll keep in touch with Kristin so I'll know how things go."

"If you like. Thank you for the services you provided. It helped in the transition period."

She put on her coat, buttoning it slowly. "Was your trip to Savannah fun?"

He glanced at her and shrugged. She heard Kristin talking to Tommy as they entered the kitchen. Buddy leaned against his mistress's leg and Kristin looked up, smiling when she saw Mac.

"There's your daddy. Run give him a hug," she said, putting Tommy down.

Sam watched the familiar scene. Mac scooped up his son

and hugged him gently. Settling him on his arm, he told Tommy to tell Sam goodbye.

"Bye-bye," Tommy said, smiling.

Sam whispered goodbye and left, tears stinging in her eyes. She really had no reason to ever see the McAlhenys again.

Two weeks later Sam entered her home to silence. She knew Charlene and Alice had their first evening quilting class, working on one of the patterns Charlene had designed. Monica had told them twenty-three women signed up for the six-week class.

She ran upstairs to change and then entered the kitchen to see how much work had been done that day. Because of a cancellation, Mac's carpenter friend had been able to start renovations to their kitchen ahead of the original schedule. The roof repair had been paid off and with Charlene's recent check from the sale of two quilts, they had enough to start on the kitchen.

The back wall had been framed and insulation installed. She could feel the difference in temperature already. There was still plenty to do, but at least the elements would stay at bay.

The mail had been placed on the counter in the kitchen. Sam glanced through it, her eye stopping on one with a National Park Service logo. She opened it and read through, not understanding at first. She'd been accepted for a volunteer project at Mesa Verde National Park starting in March and lasting for six weeks. She stared at the letter. She hadn't signed up for volunteer work. She had sent out inquiries about job openings. Was this a way to get her foot into the door?

But starting in March? That was less than a month away. She couldn't just leave her job for six weeks.

Or—maybe she could. There was vacation time accrued and leave of absence possibilities. She clutched the letter to her heart. At last, she was going to start doing what she wanted all her life! She spun around. There was no one to share this with. Charlene wouldn't be home for hours.

Spotting the phone, Sam crossed without thinking and dialed Mac's home number.

"Hello?"

Just hearing his voice after two weeks was wonderful. "Mac, it's Sam. I'm going to Mesa Verde!" she said excitedly. "I've been selected for a volunteer's position. I don't know how exactly, but it starts in three weeks and lasts for six. I'm going west!"

"I'm happy for you, Sam. I know how much you have wanted this. What will you be doing?"

"It says working on repairing and marking trails in time for the busy summer season. The park provides a place for me to stay and meals. I can't believe it. I applied for jobs, but haven't heard about any of those. But this is an honest-to-goodness official letter. It details when I should arrive, how I'll get there from the airport, everything."

"Who knows, maybe there will be a job opening while you're there and you can segue over and continue," he suggested, his tone polite.

"I thought I'd need my college degree first."

"Maybe not. I'm sure there are jobs to be had without one. Once hired, you can work your way up."

"I'm so excited. I wanted someone to share it with. I'll send you a postcard from Colorado."

"Tommy would love that," Mac said.

The bubble burst. Of course Mac wouldn't want to hear from her. She was lucky he was as cordial as he was on the phone. She hadn't any illusions she had hurt him with her refusal, especially since Kristin was working out so well. For a moment she wished he'd protest her leaving. Say something to show he cared for her beyond child care for Tommy.

Sam had spoken to Kristin only a few days ago. She loved the position and had already had her daughter over.

Mac had his future secured, so he had no reason to continue a friendship with her. His friends traveled in circles much more exalted than her own. He'd have no trouble finding women companions. If she had any doubts, the fact he hadn't phoned or dropped by proved it to her.

She'd missed him more than she'd anticipated. Every day she hoped one of the phone calls at work was Mac calling and talking about his day, or about Tommy. Or even a call in the evening. None came.

"I'll send him one every week. I've got to go. Bye." She could scarcely talk with the strain of tears in her throat. She was getting what she wanted, so why did she feel like crying?

Mac heard the connection end and slowly hung up. Hearing her voice was bittersweet. He was happy she liked the volunteer position. With Charlene's help, he'd applied in Sam's name. It wasn't the ultimate job she hoped for, but it was a chance for her to realize her dreams earlier than waiting until she received her degree. He'd arranged for help at the Beale Foundation in her absence and sweetened the deal with a hefty donation. Her boss was sorry for her to go, but wouldn't stand in her way. As she'd find out when asking for time off.

Mac closed his eyes, seeing her face so clearly. She probably sparkled with happiness at the news. He could picture her dark eyes lighting up in delight. He'd already heard the exhilaration in her tone. She was probably already calling for airline reservations and thinking of which clothes to take, and dancing around the kitchen in excitement.

He wished he was going with her.

No, he wished she was staying and marrying him. Wished she'd put him ahead of her teenage dreams.

But she'd made her choice abundantly clear. That wasn't in the cards. He'd get used to it someday—he hoped.

In the meantime, he wanted her to be happy. It wasn't her fault she didn't love him. He still wished her the very best life had to offer, and if this was her life's dream, why not get it? Except for Chris's death, he'd gotten most of what he set out to do. And he hoped he had another forty years or so of growing his company and meeting the challenges ahead. Watching Tommy become a man. For a very short time he'd thought there could be more children, if he married Sam.

Knowing her had opened his mind to the possibility of finding another woman someday whom he'd fall in love with. Maybe.

He rose and went to find Tommy. Who was he kidding? He had been lucky enough to find two women in his life he cared enough about to want share his life with. He wouldn't find a third. And right now he didn't want to. He could picture Sam in every room, making changes, bringing life to a rather somber home. And to a man who had thought life was over except for his son.

The past two weeks had seemed empty. Alice had stayed until Kristin was fully ready to take over. He'd talked to Charlene twice. Did Sam know that? But he hadn't heard Sam's voice or seen her once. He missed her. How would he last another forty years without her?

"Mac? It's Charlene again."

"Anything wrong?" he asked. He hadn't talked to Sam's sister in the weeks since she told him about the volunteer job.

"Not exactly. Sam's leaving in the morning. Her flight leaves at nine. I can't make the airport. I'm doing so much better about getting out in public and all, but I'm not up to that."

"Your classes are doing well. Mrs. Horton came by the other day to see Tommy and told Kristin how well things are going. I'm glad for you, Charlene."

"Thanks. It's not as easy as others think it ought to be. But I can't go to the airport. And I want someone to see Sam off. You know, I think she won't be coming home. Once there, she's sure to find a job that will pay enough to live on. I know she'll be back for visits, but I just have a feeling she won't ever be living here again. Unless— Never mind. Can you take her, please?"

"Me? She doesn't want to see me," he protested. Yet even as he said it, he thought of seeing her again. One last time before she left Atlanta. How could he refuse?

"Forget I said that. Whether she does or doesn't, I'll take her. What time should I pick her up?" he asked.

"Oh, that would be perfect. She was getting a cab, so she didn't have to park her car at the airport. She needs to be there early. So I'd say around seven."

"I'll be there by seven."

"Thanks, Mac. You know, I'm sorry it didn't work out between the two of you. I thought she— Never mind. Thanks for taking her. I know it won't be easy. But I didn't know who else to ask."

So the next morning he'd pick up Sam, take her to the flight that would whisk her west—where her heart lay. He'd say a final goodbye to the only other woman he'd ever want to marry and return home hoping to find the strength to go it alone.

He'd never been able to say farewell to Chris. She'd gone so fast.

At least Sam was healthy and happy. She'd be free for the first time since her parents' death. Not burdened with her sister or that old house. And not a young boy who had years to go before being grown.

Sam carried her bags to the front door, wishing Charlene had not arranged for Mac to take her to the airport. A cab would have been fine.

Her sister glided into the entryway. "He won't be here for another few moments. Why don't you at least have some toast."

"Can't eat a thing." She was nervous. Not about going to Colorado, but about seeing Mac again. She'd thought about him endlessly since that last night at his place. Wished a dozen times or more to pick up the phone to call him, hear his voice. She missed little Tommy, too, nearly as much as she missed Mac. When she'd called to share the news about her new opportunity, she'd felt as if she'd been wrapped in home hearing him speak.

Wiping her palms against her slacks, she looked out the side glass by the door. No car yet.

Winter was starting to fade. In a few weeks, the azaleas would be in full bloom, flowering trees would burst into color. She'd be back in time to catch some of the late spring-time blossoms. What were western mountain springs like?

She saw the car turn into the driveway.

"He's here." She could hardly wait to see him again.

"I'm not sure I'm ready for you to leave," Charlene said suddenly.

Sam turned, startled. "What?"

"Forget I said that. Alice will be here tonight and moving the rest of her things in by the end of the week. It's just—"

"I know," Sam said, giving her sister a hug. It had been the two of them against the world ever since their parents died. Now she was leaving. Life as they knew it was changing again.

"But you'll be just fine." Sam truly believed that. Charlene had blossomed beyond her wildest dreams these last weeks. Sam wouldn't have left if she hadn't known her sister would manage perfectly well with her gone.

"I know it. And you, too. You'll finally get what you've always wanted," Charlene said, but her eyes filled with tears and her smile was wobbly.

"I guess," Sam said, feeling her own throat tighten with emotion.

"Isn't it what you've always wanted?" her sister asked sharply.

The knock on the door saved her from answering. She opened it and saw Mac. He looked tired and thinner than she remembered, but he was still the most gorgeous man she'd ever seen.

"Hi." She wanted to throw herself into his arms. Have him pull her close and kiss her like he had before.

"Ready to go?" he asked.

"Yes. I have these two bags." She drew on her jacket and gave Charlene another kiss. "I'll call from Denver."

"I'm happy for you, Sam," Charlene said. "Do what makes your heart sing."

Mac stowed her bags in the trunk and held the passenger door open for her. She slipped in, fastening her seat belt before he could get behind the wheel.

"I appreciate your giving me a ride. If you drop me at Departures, you shouldn't even be late for work," she said brightly. She hoped he wouldn't hear the nervousness in her voice. There was so much she wanted to say. That apology still needed to be voiced. Could she do it before she left?

"I plan to go as far as security will allow," he said. "We can wait there until your flight is called."

"You don't have to," she said, hoping he would. Now that the moment was here, she was scared. What if working in the national parks didn't prove to be the most wonderful job in the world? What if she couldn't do it? What if—

"Tommy sent you this," he said, handing her a wrapped package. By the way the paper was bunched up at one end and barely touching at the other, she suspected Tommy had been the one to wrap it. She tore off the paper. A small truck sat in her palm.

"It's his favorite. He wanted you to have it on your trip."

"Thank him for me," she said, clutching it tightly. Her throat was tight again. She blinked her eyes and stared straight ahead. She should have gone by the house when Mac was at work to see Tommy before she left.

Mac handed her a card with his name, home address and private phone number written on it.

"For those postcards you're sending."

She smiled and nodded, feeling his warmth still on the card. "I already have it, but I'll keep this, too," she said, slipping it into her pocket.

Traffic was heavy and conversation was light. He parked in short-term parking and carried one bag while Sam insisted on carrying the other. Once the luggage was checked, he offered to buy her a cup of coffee.

"No, thanks. I'm sure I'll get some on the flight." She wouldn't be able to drink a thing with him. Her nerves stretched tighter. They walked to the security area. The line was short.

"You don't need to stay," she said, glancing at the line and then back at Mac. "I'll go on through and head for the gate." She rolled and unrolled her ticket folder. "Thank you for bringing me," she said.

"No problem. Enjoy yourself."

She glanced at him briefly, then gazed ahead, gearing up her courage. "Mac, I wanted to apologize for my rude response to your proposal of marriage. Not that it excuses anything, but you caught me by surprise and I just blurted out words without thinking."

"Sam."

She looked up at him.

"Have the best life you can. Grab hold and wring it for everything it's worth. Your dream is coming true. That's a gift not everyone gets."

Mac kissed her, drawing her close against him, holding her as if she were precious and fragile. Then he broke the kiss and smiled at her. "Bon voyage, Madam Ranger."

"Goodbye." She turned and headed through security, resisting the urge to turn to see him one last time as she walked away. It was the hardest thing Samantha had ever done.

CHAPTER TEN

DEAR Mac. It's more spectacular than I imagined. I can see forever when I'm on top of a mountain. The air is so clean and clear. There are areas where I don't see trees for acres and acres of windswept land. And then thick lodgepole pines grow so close together I can't imagine walking through them.

She stared at the words. Stupid. She bunched up the postcard and tossed it into the trash. The third ruined one tonight. Leaning back in her bunk, Sam gazed at the wooden ceiling. The bunkhouse where the volunteers were housed was rustic. Built of the lodgepole pines she was trying to describe, it gave the western ambiance she'd so yearned for.

How to convey all she was feeling in a postcard?

And why should Mac care? She'd said no. End of relationship.

Rolling on her side, she blinked back tears. She did so not want it to be the end. She had achieved her heart's desire and it wasn't proving to be what she thought it would be. Instead of throwing herself into her tasks each day, she kept wondering what Mac was doing—if he was attending some charity event where he'd meet someone new. Fall for another woman who would not hesitate a moment to accept his proposal and then share his home and help raise Tommy. Maybe even have more children.

A pang of remorse hit her—again. Why had she said no so quickly? Maybe she should have asked for time to decide.

Kristin was managing fine, just as Sam had predicted. Sam had spoken to her a few times using the TDD service of the phone company after Kristin started working for Mac. Everything sounded like it was a good match. Sam had called once from the main lodge after she'd arrived in Mesa Verde. Mac had not been home, so she had called back to have a short chat with Kristin.

When she asked after Mac and Tommy, Kristin merely said they were doing fine.

Sam missed them both with an ache that constantly surprised her. More even than she missed her own sister.

She'd called Charlene a couple of times as well, but it was hard to talk for long. With no cell service in the mountains the volunteers had to use the pay phone at the lodge. Standing by the outside phone, in the cold, wasn't conducive to lengthy conversations. Charlene remained enthusiastic about the quilting classes. She'd told Sam about an offer from a pattern publisher for one of her patterns. She bubbled with joy. Sam felt a moment of envy.

When Charlene asked how she liked Colorado, she was honest in saying it was beautiful. But she didn't tell Charlene how lonely she was. Her friends weren't here. Everyone participating in the volunteer program had jobs and homes and friends scattered around the U.S. She was the only one who had declared an interest in doing this full-time. To most, it was a change, a special vacation this year. Something different. They'd be returning to their normal lives when the six weeks ended.

She didn't know what she'd be doing next.

She missed hearing about Mac, seeing him. She sat up and picked another postcard, wishing she could just talk to him for a few minutes. Well, why not? Tossing the postcard on the bed, she hopped off her bunk and bundled up. She'd try again. It was after eight in Georgia, so Tommy would be in bed. It was Mac's voice she yearned to hear, surely he'd be home by now.

It was still light as she walked from the sleeping quarters to the main lodge. No one was using the pay phone so she stepped up and began feeding it change. The phone rang four times before clicking to an answering machine. She debated leaving a message. But what would she say?

Hanging up, she called Charlene.

"Hi, what's up?" she said when her sister answered.

"Not much, still working with Monica and loving it. How about you?"

"We did a lot of work on one of the trails today. It's hard physical labor, but really satisfying and the views are spectacular. I can't get over how different this part of the country is."

"I bet. One day I'll have to get out there and see for myself."

They chatted for a few minutes then Sam asked, "Have you heard anything from Mac?"

"No, should I have?'

Sam sighed softly. "No, no reason. I just wondered. I tried calling him earlier, but it rang to the answering machine."

"Did you want to tell him something?"

"No, um, I just was going to tell him about Mesa Verde. Glad your classes are going so well. I've got to run."

"Thanks for calling, Sam."

Sam hung up and gazed around her. She did enjoy being here. But she also began to realize it was a perfect vacation. Just like the others in the group. She wanted to return home when the six weeks was over. She wanted to see Mac and Tommy and maybe even attend one of Charlene's classes to see how she handled it.

She thought about the people she worked with at the Beale Foundation, hoping some of the men and women she placed were doing as well as Kristin was. Wondering if Timothy had found more sponsors for their grant program.

Mostly, she thought, as she slowly walked back to the bunkhouse, she wanted to see Mac McAlheny. To hear how his day had gone. To visit the zoo or someplace else with him and Tommy. To hold hands. Kiss. Share meals. Share a bed.

She blinked. Gazing over the beautiful landscape, Sam realized she loved Mac. She probably had from the first moment he'd rescued her from the drunk at the Black and White Ball.

She hugged herself and stared across the land. "I love Mac," she said aloud, astonished. The wind carried the sound away. The breeze swept through her, chilling her in the colder evening air. "He never said he loved me, but that doesn't change anything. I love him." For a moment she wished he'd appear and ask her to marry him again. Or that she could change the past and realize sooner that dreams sometimes aren't meant to come true. That life changes and new dreams replace old ones. The reality was she loved Mac and wanted to spend the rest of her life with him. In Atlanta, vacationing in the west, doing everything together. With Tommy and maybe if they were lucky, with several more children to fill up the house and have it ring with laughter—and love.

"He never said he loved me," Sam said once again to the sky as if to convince herself.

An old axiom her mother often said sprang to mind. Actions speak louder than words.

He had asked her to marry him. Was it for more reasons than simply because he needed a nanny for Tommy? Had she misread the entire situation?

She felt slightly sick at the thought. She couldn't have.

Yet the man had a ton of money. He could hire three nannies if he wanted. But she was the one he'd asked to marry him.

She turned and went back to the phone, fumbling the money in her haste to get the call through. She had to talk to him. See if there was more than she'd thought. See if she could get a second chance.

She placed the second call to Mac's home. When the answering machine clicked on, she rushed into speech.

"Mac, it's Sam. Sorry you aren't home. I really wanted to talk with you. I'll be away from a phone most of tomorrow working, but will try you again about this time tomorrow evening. I hope you'll be home." She held on another few seconds, but couldn't find the words to say what she felt. "So, maybe I'll talk to you then." Slowly she hung up and slowly walked to one of the overlooks and gazed off into the growing twilight. It would be dark soon. The stars would be magnificent in the night sky without the ambient light of cities. The pinpoints of light ranged from faint to bright. She would never tire of looking at the night sky here. Or the endless scenery. Or feeling the dry breeze caress her skin—even if it was cold. In summer it would be a pleasant relief from the heat. She did like this vast space. She had felt she was contributing as she worked on the trails.

But was it enough to build a life on? Her friends were in Atlanta. Her only family was there. And the man and boy she loved were there. How could she have thought she could jettison all that and build a life so far away?

Finally, growing cold, she returned to the bunkhouse.

The next day it rained. The volunteers met in one of the conference rooms at the lodge and the rangers gave more information on the history of the park, what was known of the ancients who had built the cave dwellings. Pictures of the ruins were displayed and artifacts explained. It was fascinating, but Sam couldn't focus fully on the presentation. Glancing at her watch again, she was dismayed to find it was only five minutes later than the last time she'd looked. She was impatiently waiting for when she could phone Mac again.

How long would the day stretch out?

At lunch, as she listened to the conversation swirl around her, she considered calling now, while he was still at work. Only, she didn't want to talk to him there. She wanted time enough and privacy. She had to wait. But patience was proving hard to come by.

She wasn't sure what she was going to say, but if there was any chance she could renew their relationship, she wanted it. Mostly she wanted to hear his voice.

One of the women who worked in the office came in the lunchroom and headed for Sam's table.

"You have a visitor," she said, resting her hand on Sam's shoulder.

Sam looked up in surprise. "I do?"

"Waiting by the fireplace in the main room. Lucky you," she said with a friendly smile. She waved at the others and left.

Sam excused herself from the table and headed out. No sooner had she stepped into the main room than she wondered if her eyes were playing tricks.

"Mac?" She wanted to fly across the room right into his arms. But she drew a deep breath and walked across the space slowly. He watched her as she approached. He wore dark cords and the jacket he'd worn to the zoo. Her heart began to race.

"What are you doing here?" she asked.

"I was in the neighborhood and thought I'd stop by."

"I'm glad you did," she said, drinking in the sight of him. Her fingers still longed to trace that dimple, to thread through his hair. Her eyes could drink him in all day. Whatever he was doing here was fine with her.

"Come sit down by the fire," she said, leading the way to an empty sofa before the cavernous fireplace that contained a couple of logs burning merrily. She sat on the edge of the leather furniture. He shed his jacket and sat beside her.

"Are you liking it?" he asked.

She nodded. She should say something. She felt like an idiot.

"It was hard to tell from all those postcards you've sent," he said.

"I know, I should have sent more than that one to Tommy, but I was having trouble writing what I wanted to say." She wondered what he'd think of all the crumpled ones in her wastebasket right now.

"Too busy every minute?"

"Too uncertain what to say," she replied.

He started to say something, then shook his head. "So tell me about your day. Obviously you're not working in the rain."

"We might have if a project had been important enough. But we're restoring some of the trails and today was too wet to work effectively. So we've spent the morning in a class-room setting learning more about the park. Most days, when the weather's good, we're out early, working all day until time for dinner."

She went on to describe their tasks and how she was learning so much. She tried to infuse her voice with enthu-siasm but trailed off after a minute.

"I can't believe you're here!" *Tell him now!* her inner voice urged. But she couldn't find the right way to open the subject.

"I won't be staying long. I just wanted to see you since I was close. See how you were doing."

"I'm fine. I still can't believe I was offered the position, but I've met a lot of people from all around the country. We all work well together."

"It paid off, then," he said.

"What did?"

"Getting you the job."

"What?" She stared at him. "I don't understand."

He shrugged. "I thought Charlene would have explained.

She helped me fill out the application because she knew all the personal information. That's why you were chosen. I thought once here, it'd be easier to get a permanent job than applying from Atlanta. They'd know you, what you can do."

She felt her heart drop. He hadn't wasted any time after her refusal getting her out of Atlanta. He didn't love her. He had moved on. And had practically sent her away.

"Oh. I didn't know." It hurt. She'd been bubbling with possibilities since she'd realized how much she loved him. Now it was as if he had shut the door on a future together when he told her that.

This changed everything. Had she been given a second chance? Was there a possibility he might still want to marry her? It was so important, she had to do it just right. But what if she had misread every indication? What should she say? Just blurt out, *I've changed my mind—I love you and want to marry you?* What if he'd changed his in the meantime? She bit her lower lip.

"Where's Tommy?" Great, bring up the excuse she'd used to refuse his proposal. Pangs of guilt flooded through her. "I miss him," she said. How could she ever have thought he might be a burden? He was a precious child bringing joy and delight to everyone who met him. She'd thought about their evenings together when lying lonely on her bunk at nights.

"Staying with my parents for a few days. I pick him up tomorrow night. He's doing well with Kristin. She's teaching him sign language."

She nodded. "I called your house last night, but there was no answer." Tension rose. How could she broach the subject? Time was ticking away. Would he stay long enough for her to say what was in her heart? It might have been easier on the phone. But she wouldn't trade these moments together for anything. She wished she dared reach out to touch him. Wished she knew the future, knew if he'd be open to building a relationship with her.

"I wasn't home, obviously. Kristin had the evenings to herself with us both gone. Maybe she went out with her daughter."

Sam nodded again, gazing at the fire. She cleared her throat. Maybe something would come out if she'd just start speaking. If she could think with the blood pounding through her. Her throat was dry. Words evaporated before she could voice them.

He stood. "I'll give Charlene an update when I get home. She'll want to know you're looking good and love this."

Sam stood and reached out to hold his arm. "You just got here. You can't leave." Time was running out, and she felt as dumb as dirt. Rubbing one palm against her jeans, she tried to come up with the words that would keep him here.

"I wanted to see you. Make sure you were happy. I've a long drive back to Colorado Springs," he said, taking her hand in one of his, brushing the back with his thumb.

"Thanks for coming, Mac. It's good to see you," she said, tightening her grip, wishing she never had to let him go. Instead, when he released her a moment later, she let her arm fall to her side. She remained standing near the sofa, watching him cross the vast lodge lobby. Watching as he walked away. She blinked back sudden tears.

He'd dropped by because he was in the neighborhood. Not because he'd come especially to see her.

Only—Mesa Verde wasn't in any neighborhood. It was a destination in itself. And it was more than a five-hour drive back to Colorado Springs. No one came that far just to say hi.

"Wait," she called, suddenly thinking of something. Not much, but it would hold him here another few moments. Would something brilliant come to mind by then?

He turned and waited while she hurried over.

"Can you pick me up at the airport when I get back home?" she asked.

He looked surprised. "You're coming back?"

"Why wouldn't I? I live in Atlanta."

"Only until you get a job here. Charlene said she didn't expect you back."

"She did? Huh. I didn't know that. Anyway, I don't have a job here and don't expect an offer for one."

"Oh, sweetheart, I'm sorry. Something will turn up, just wait."

The word *sweetheart* about melted her heart. The look of compassion in his eyes touched her.

"It's not quite like I thought it would be," she said slowly. Hoping she was doing this right. Please, let it come out right.

"Why is that?"

"I love it here. It's beautiful. I'm making a difference in the trail. All summer people from all over the world will be coming to walk on the trail I'm helping to repair."

"And you want to be here to see that," he said.

She shook her head slowly. "I want to be where the people I love are."

Mac didn't say anything and her heart dropped. He had never said he loved her. She had never told him she loved him. But these weeks apart had shown her as nothing else could how much she missed him. How much she'd yearned to hear his voice, to know he was safe and happy. To be part of his life.

"I want to be where you are, Mac," she said in a rush.

He dropped his jacket and reached for her, pulling her into his arms and kissing her like he had before. Those wonderful kisses that rocked her world. Sam couldn't say a word, so she just held on and kissed him back.

Endless minutes later he pulled back a scant inch. "I never thought I'd hear you say that, Sam. If you don't want marriage, we can be friends, do things together, though I love you so much it'll be hell on earth if you don't say you'll marry me. I thought I could do this when you said no.

Send you on your way and be glad you were happy. But these last weeks have been horrible. As bad as when Chris died. I never thought I'd fall in love again, or so completely that my life isn't my own anymore. But I have. With you. Oh, my love, say you'll share my life until we are both ancient and beyond."

"You love me? You never said."

"I didn't?" he asked.

She shook her head. "I love you, too. Only I was too stupid or too blind to realize it until I got here. I thought I ruined everything. Coming here is exactly like I thought it would be. But I'm not like I thought I'd be. I can't stop thinking about you. Wishing I was with you. To cook dinner together or take Tommy to the park or tuck him in bed together. To talk about everything under the sun. I want to be with you."

"Will you marry me?"

Before she could respond, he put a finger across her lips. "Think about what you want to say. I can't take another rejection like last time."

She threw back her head and laughed, then hugged him tightly. She couldn't even imagine what had gone through her mind that fateful morning. How could she have been so blind to her true feelings?

"I might have answered differently if you'd started that proposal with an I love you. Oh, Mac, I so love you! I would be very honored to be your wife. I'm sorry for that refusal. How dumb can one woman be? But I had this dream for so long, I didn't realize when it changed. Learning about these temporary volunteer positions is great. When I get the urge, I'll volunteer. The rest of the time, I want to be with you. Raise Tommy. Have a half dozen kids of our own. Watch Charlene take off. But mostly—always—to be with you."

"That can be arranged," he said before he kissed her again. A kiss that warmed her to her toes, and assured her their future would always be bright together.

MILLS & BOON®
Pure reading pleasure™

NOVEMBER 2008 HARDBACK TITLES

ROMANCE

The Billionaire's Bride of Vengeance   978 0 263 20382 0
Miranda Lee
The Santangeli Marriage *Sara Craven*   978 0 263 20383 7
The Spaniard's Virgin Housekeeper   978 0 263 20384 4
Diana Hamilton
The Greek Tycoon's Reluctant Bride *Kate Hewitt*   978 0 263 20385 1
Innocent Mistress, Royal Wife *Robyn Donald*   978 0 263 20386 8
Taken for Revenge, Bedded for Pleasure   978 0 263 20387 5
India Grey
The Billionaire Boss's Innocent Bride   978 0 263 20388 2
Lindsay Armstrong
The Billionaire's Defiant Wife *Amanda Browning*   978 0 263 20389 9
Nanny to the Billionaire's Son *Barbara McMahon*   978 0 263 20390 5
Cinderella and the Sheikh *Natasha Oakley*   978 0 263 20391 2
Promoted: Secretary to Bride! *Jennie Adams*   978 0 263 20392 9
The Black Sheep's Proposal *Patricia Thayer*   978 0 263 20393 6
The Snow-Kissed Bride *Linda Goodnight*   978 0 263 20394 3
The Rancher's Runaway Princess *Donna Alward*   978 0 263 20395 0
The Greek Doctor's New-Year Baby *Kate Hardy*   978 0 263 20396 7
The Wife He's Been Waiting For *Dianne Drake*   978 0 263 20397 4

HISTORICAL

The Captain's Forbidden Miss *Margaret McPhee*   978 0 263 20216 8
The Earl and the Hoyden *Mary Nichols*   978 0 263 20217 5
From Governess to Society Bride *Helen Dickson*   978 0 263 20218 2

MEDICAL™

The Heart Surgeon's Secret Child *Meredith Webber*   978 0 263 19918 5
The Midwife's Little Miracle *Fiona McArthur*   978 0 263 19919 2
The Single Dad's New-Year Bride *Amy Andrews*   978 0 263 19920 8
Posh Doc Claims His Bride *Anne Fraser*   978 0 263 19921 5

MILLS & BOON®
Pure reading pleasure™

NOVEMBER 2008 LARGE PRINT TITLES

ROMANCE

Bought for Revenge, Bedded for Pleasure *Emma Darcy*	978 0 263 20090 4
Forbidden: The Billionaire's Virgin Princess *Lucy Monroe*	978 0 263 20091 1
The Greek Tycoon's Convenient Wife *Sharon Kendrick*	978 0 263 20092 8
The Marciano Love-Child *Melanie Milburne*	978 0 263 20093 5
Parents in Training *Barbara McMahon*	978 0 263 20094 2
Newlyweds of Convenience *Jessica Hart*	978 0 263 20095 9
The Desert Prince's Proposal *Nicola Marsh*	978 0 263 20096 6
Adopted: Outback Baby *Barbara Hannay*	978 0 263 20097 3

HISTORICAL

The Virtuous Courtesan *Mary Brendan*	978 0 263 20172 7
The Homeless Heiress *Anne Herries*	978 0 263 20173 4
Rebel Lady, Convenient Wife *June Francis*	978 0 263 20174 1

MEDICAL™

Nurse Bride, Bayside Wedding *Gill Sanderson*	978 0 263 19986 4
Billionaire Doctor, Ordinary Nurse *Carol Marinelli*	978 0 263 19987 1
The Sheikh Surgeon's Baby *Meredith Webber*	978 0 263 19988 8
The Outback Doctor's Surprise Bride *Amy Andrews*	978 0 263 19989 5
A Wedding at Limestone Coast *Lucy Clark*	978 0 263 19990 1
The Doctor's Meant-To-Be Marriage *Janice Lynn*	978 0 263 19991 8

MILLS & BOON®
Pure reading pleasure™

DECEMBER 2008 HARDBACK TITLES

ROMANCE

The Ruthless Magnate's Virgin Mistress *Lynne Graham*	978 0 263 20398 1
The Greek's Forced Bride *Michelle Reid*	978 0 263 20399 8
The Sheikh's Rebellious Mistress *Sandra Marton*	978 0 263 20400 1
The Prince's Waitress Wife *Sarah Morgan*	978 0 263 20401 8
Bought for the Sicilian Billionaire's Bed *Sharon Kendrick*	978 0 263 20402 5
Count Maxime's Virgin *Susan Stephens*	978 0 263 20403 2
The Italian's Ruthless Baby Bargain *Margaret Mayo*	978 0 263 20404 9
Valenti's One-Month Mistress *Sabrina Philips*	978 0 263 20405 6
The Australian's Society Bride *Margaret Way*	978 0 263 20406 3
The Royal Marriage Arrangement *Rebecca Winters*	978 0 263 20407 0
Two Little Miracles *Caroline Anderson*	978 0 263 20408 7
Manhattan Boss, Diamond Proposal *Trish Wylie*	978 0 263 20409 4
Her Valentine Blind Date *Raye Morgan*	978 0 263 20410 0
The Bridesmaid and the Billionaire *Shirley Jump*	978 0 263 20411 7
Children's Doctor, Society Bride *Joanna Neil*	978 0 263 20412 4
Outback Doctor, English Bride *Leah Martyn*	978 0 263 20413 1

HISTORICAL

Marrying the Mistress *Juliet Landon*	978 0 263 20219 9
To Deceive a Duke *Amanda McCabe*	978 0 263 20220 5
Knight of Grace *Sophia James*	978 0 263 20221 2

MEDICAL™

The Heart Surgeon's Baby Surprise *Meredith Webber*	978 0 263 19922 2
A Wife for the Baby Doctor *Josie Metcalfe*	978 0 263 19923 9
The Royal Doctor's Bride *Jessica Matthews*	978 0 263 19924 6
Surgeon Boss, Surprise Dad *Janice Lynn*	978 0 263 19925 3

MILLS & BOON®
Pure reading pleasure™

DECEMBER 2008 LARGE PRINT TITLES

ROMANCE

Title	Author	ISBN
Hired: The Sheikh's Secretary Mistress	*Lucy Monroe*	978 0 263 20098 0
The Billionaire's Blackmailed Bride	*Jacqueline Baird*	978 0 263 20099 7
The Sicilian's Innocent Mistress	*Carole Mortimer*	978 0 263 20100 0
The Sheikh's Defiant Bride	*Sandra Marton*	978 0 263 20101 7
Wanted: Royal Wife and Mother	*Marion Lennox*	978 0 263 20102 4
The Boss's Unconventional Assistant *Jennie Adams*		978 0 263 20103 1
Inherited: Instant Family	*Judy Christenberry*	978 0 263 20104 8
The Prince's Secret Bride	*Raye Morgan*	978 0 263 20105 5

HISTORICAL

Title	Author	ISBN
Miss Winthorpe's Elopement	*Christine Merrill*	978 0 263 20175 8
The Rake's Unconventional Mistress *Juliet Landon*		978 0 263 20176 5
Rags-to-Riches Bride	*Mary Nichols*	978 0 263 20177 2

MEDICAL™

Title	Author	ISBN
Single Dad Seeks a Wife	*Melanie Milburne*	978 0 263 19992 5
Her Four-Year Baby Secret	*Alison Roberts*	978 0 263 19993 2
Country Doctor, Spring Bride	*Abigail Gordon*	978 0 263 19994 9
Marrying the Runaway Bride	*Jennifer Taylor*	978 0 263 19995 6
The Midwife's Baby	*Fiona McArthur*	978 0 263 19996 3
The Fatherhood Miracle	*Margaret Barker*	978 0 263 19997 0